THE MONEY CLUB

A High Desert Cozy Mystery - Book 9

BY

DIANNE HARMAN

Published by: Dianne Harman
www.dianneharman.com

Interior, cover design and website by
Vivek Rajan

ISBN: 9781088899717

CONTENTS

ACKNOWLEDGMENTS

Several years ago, my husband and I took a vacation in the Russian River area of Northern California. While we were there, we heard many references to The Bohemian Club. We learned this is a group of wealthy men who belong to a private club in San Francisco and also maintain a compound near where we were staying.

I became fascinated with the concept of a private location – in this case called The Bohemian Grove – where these men came annually to share information and take part in discussions led by national and global leaders, even past U.S. presidents.

The Money Club, as described in this book, is loosely based on that group, although, as always, it is a work of fiction and takes place in the Palm Springs area, not Northern California. I hope you enjoy the read as much as I enjoyed the research and the write!

As always, thanks to my dedicated support team. I so appreciate everything you do to make me look good and my books bestsellers!

And to Tom, for your unending support. Thank you.

Win FREE Paperbacks every week!

Go to www.dianneharman.com/freepaperback.html and get your FREE copies of Dianne's books and favorite recipes immediately by signing up for her newsletter.

Once you've signed up for her newsletter you're eligible to win three paperbacks. One lucky winner is picked every week. Hurry before the offer ends!

PROLOGUE

It was a pleasant warm afternoon in High Desert, a small town about thirty miles north of Palm Springs. Marty Morgan and her sister, Laura, were relaxing in the courtyard of the four-house compound that Laura owned which was located on the edge of the desert that Laura owned.

"Be back in a sec, Laura, I can hear my phone ringing," Marty said to Laura, who was stretched out on a lounge chair, checking her email messages. "I'm coming, I'm coming," Marty said to herself as she hurried inside from the compound's courtyard to answer her phone.

"This is Marty Morgan. May I help you?" she asked.

"Only if you promise me no one is dead or gonna' be dead," the voice, which she recognized as Carl Mitchell's, said. Carl was the owner of an antique store in Palm Springs called Ye Olde Antique Shoppe, and often assisted Marty when she was doing a personal property appraisal for clients.

"Carl, that I can promise you. How are you, and did you ever hear from Miles Reed?" she asked, referring to an entertainer they had recently met while Marty was involved in solving the murder of Jimmy Joseph, the legendary music man of Las Vegas and the world.

"As a matter of fact, I did. I just received a very nice note from him thanking me for sending him the Elvis Presley jacket. He says he wears it in one of the shows he's doing in Las Vegas and considers it to be his lucky talisman."

"Well, you had a feeling it was right for him, and it was. Good thing someone brought it into your antique shop."

"I know, and that's why I'm calling. One of my best customers was in today and needs an appraisal on some fantastic pieces of art and other things I've sold him over the years. I recommended you. I expect you'll hear from him pretty soon. He said his insurance company has been calling him almost daily after he gave them a list of the art pieces and a rough estimate of their value."

"Actually, Carl, I think he beat you to the punch. If his name is Jerry Jessup, I just had a call from him, and as a matter of fact, he and I are meeting tomorrow at the Casa Flores. It's not all that far from where I live, but I have a question for you."

"Shoot," Carl said

"You have an appraisal business in addition to your antique shop, and considering how often I've hired you to help me, you know that I think you're an excellent appraiser. Question is, why aren't you doing the appraisal?"

"Fair question. Problem is I'm the one who has sold the Casa pretty much everything you'll be appraising. If they suffered a loss and tried to collect from their insurance company, it could be a problem, because of my involvement as the seller and the appraisal could be called into question. They're such a good customer I didn't want to mess anything up for future sales, and I could possibly be causing problems for them in the event of a loss."

"I think you're absolutely right. It might be a grey area, and if the insurance company made trouble, it could hurt your credibility with them. Thanks for the referral."

"I hope you feel that way after you do it," Carl said ominously.

"What do you mean?" Marty asked.

"Marty, I need to talk to you about this appraisal before you do it. There are some rather interesting aspects to it. Any chance you could come by the shop this afternoon?"

"From what I'm hearing, it sounds like I better make time."

"Didn't really want to put it that way, but yes, I think that would be a good idea. When should I look for you?"

"I can be there in an hour. Say around 3:00."

"See you then."

*****

That was Carl," Marty said to Laura as she returned to the large courtyard. The large collection of plants in the courtyard was Laura's hobby. All sorts of desert and non-desert plants were in hanging baskets and pots scattered around the courtyard. She'd carefully hung strands of tiny twinkling lights in the trees, and at night the courtyard looked like a magical fairyland.

"He wants to see me this afternoon about an appraisal I'm doing tomorrow."

Duke, Marty's black Labrador retriever, and Patron, her white boxer, were both stretched out in the early afternoon sun, enjoying the peace and quiet of just being with Marty and Laura. However, that peace came to an abrupt end when Patron began to growl and the hair along his back stood on end, always a sign that he sensed something was wrong.

Marty looked over at Laura and then back at Patron. "Easy boy, easy," she said, knowing it was probably in vain. It had been Marty's experience that the only thing that calmed Patron down was Laura

3

whispering to him.

It had something to do with the psychic powers that both Laura and the dog seemed to possess. When Laura was a student at UCLA, she'd been tested and found to have legitimate psychic abilities in the form of extrasensory perception or ESP. After several incidences when Patron had sensed danger and saved both her husband, Jeff's, and her life, Marty was certain Patron possessed them as well.

Every time Marty looked at Laura and thought about her psychic abilities, she had to grin. Laura was the last person in the world anyone would look at and think she was a psychic. No crystal ball, scarf around her head, or Gypsy style clothing for her. She usually dressed very professionally in a muted color pant suit, designer shoes, and always wearing her signature diamond and gold earrings with the matching pendant and bracelet. Her look was about as far away from that of a fortune teller as one could get.

Laura stood up and walked over to Patron. She began to speak to him in a low quiet voice, and within a few moments, he calmly laid back down and went to sleep.

"What woo-woo stuff do you say to calm him down, Laura?" Marty asked. "I've tried to do what you do, and it doesn't work."

"Let's just say he and I are on the same wave length. By the way, he's going with you tomorrow when you go on that appraisal," Marty responded.

"Swell. I guess that means there's going to be a problem. Carl's already hinted to me there might be something unusual about this appraisal. Any idea what the problem might be?" Marty asked.

"No, but the whatevers you want to call them are telling me that you'll be very glad Patron is with you. I'm not getting any more than that at the moment. Just be careful, that's all I'm saying."

"Do you have any idea what those words do to my blood pressure and overall general health?" Marty asked.

"Sorry, can't help it, Sis. I only pass on what I'm given. I need to go look at a few things in my office and get back to Dick. He generously gave me the day off, but I can see a couple of things have come in that require my attention. Tell Carl I said hi."

"No, that's one thing I won't do. Ever since the wig stand incident when you walked into the dressing room area with a big knife, he lives in mortal fear of having anything to do with you. Yes, you found the missing diamond ring inside the stand, but he's still spooked by simply being around you."

"Hey, the whatevers gave me the right information, didn't they? We sure weren't getting anywhere before then. All of us figured the ring was lost and gone forever. When I suddenly knew where it was, it was all due to them."

"You know, Laura, I love you dearly, but do you know how difficult it is to have a sister who's psychic? To say nothing about having a dog who's also a psychic? Which is probably why you picked out Patron when Jeff told you to buy a puppy for me."

"No, I don't, because you clearly aren't psychic like me, but you might be right about Patron. Could just be why he called out to me when I was looking for a puppy for you. It was probably some vibe I felt. Anyway, I'll see you at dinner. Know what John's making for us tonight?"

"No, but I can guarantee you one thing. Whatever it is, the food will be good. That's why the Red Pony Food Trucks he operates are so popular and why we get to eat the terrific meals he prepares for us.

"We're like his guinea pigs, and he's always experimenting with new dishes that he tries out on us. Don't know how we got to be so lucky to have him as a resident here at the compound, but it was one lucky day when it happened."

CHAPTER ONE

Tina Quinn looked at herself in the mirror before she went into the kitchen to open the wine. Red hair cascaded to her cream-colored shoulders, accentuated by the off-the-shoulder green blouse she wore that matched her eyes. Tight white jeans and multi-colored platform sandals completed the Palm Springs "in" look. The large emerald studs she wore in her ears surrounded by pavé diamonds made her eyes look even larger.

Satisfied that Sean would be pleased by what he saw, she went into the kitchen. Sean had told her he wouldn't be able to stay for dinner because his wife, Maddie, was beginning to get suspicious at the number of nights he'd been late, far later than being the manager of the Casa Flores would warrant.

Truth be told, Tina was getting a little tired of hearing Sean make excuses why he couldn't leave Maddie. He always said he needed a little more time because his daughter, Rickie, had a problem, his wife's uncle had a heart attack, blah blah blah. It was always something.

I'm fed up with waiting any longer, she thought. *I'd planned on being married to him by now, and I certainly never expected to have to live on my divorce settlement, which has almost run out. Even though my ex is a member of The Money Club, that darn pre-nuptial agreement I signed before we were married sure came back to bite me. I should have held out for a lot more when I entered into the marriage.*

It's getting to be crunch time for me. I know it will take a while from the time Sean divorces Maddie for us to get married, but at least we could live together. The Money Club pays him enough so that he can afford to support two households. Who knows? We could even live at the Casa Flores and sell this house. That would kill my ex, Basil, and I'd consider it sweet revenge.

The more she thought about it, the more she decided that the time had come for an ultimatum. An ultimatum based on survival. Tina knew if she pressed Sean and told him she was ending the affair if he didn't leave Maddie within the week, he'd do it.

After all, hasn't he told me time after time that I'm the most important thing in the world to him? Of course he has, and of course he'd leave Maddie. I've just got to give him an ultimatum, and tonight's the night.

She hummed as she opened the wine and let it decant. She'd bought a bottle of his favorite, an Archery Summit cabernet sauvignon from Oregon. Although his job was glamorous, being around some of the wealthiest men in Southern California, the downside was that he'd developed some expensive tastes, courtesy of them, and Archery Summit wine was just one of them.

Her phone rang and she was sure it was Sean telling her he was almost there. She answered it by saying, "I'm waiting for you. Hurry up and get here."

The voice on the other end of the line said, "Tina, I'm glad you've changed your mind. I can be at your house in minutes."

It took a moment for her to register that it wasn't Sean, but instead it was her ex-boyfriend, the one she'd met after her marriage to Basil had ended. His name was Joe Barton, and he'd just gotten out of prison. She'd told him in no uncertain terms she wasn't interested in reviving their relationship, and that she'd found someone else, but every time he called, he reminded her she'd promised to wait for him while he was in prison.

She mentally berated herself for not blocking Joe's calls. It was time to make her feelings crystal clear to him. "Joe, we seem to be having a communication problem. I am not in love with you. I don't want you in my life. I don't want to see you, and if you continue to harass me by calling me, you will leave me no alternative but to call the police and report you.

"I don't know what the terms of your parole are, but I don't think your parole officer would be too thrilled about that. Anyway, there's someone else in my life, now. Don't ever call me again."

The other end of the line was silent as Joe digested what she'd just said. Joe had served a short sentence in prison for a white-collar crime, embezzling funds from his employer, funds he'd spent on winning Tina's affections. The irony was that not only had he spent time in prison because of her, now she was no longer interested in him.

Being in prison was somewhat like being in school. You learned a lot and most of what you learned would land you right back in the slammer. But when your future's on the line, you do what you have to do.

"Tina, a year of my life was spent in prison because of you, and now you're telling me you want nothing to do with me because there's someone else? Well, let's put it this way. If I can't have you neither will the someone else you referred to, and believe me, I know the people who can make that happen." The silence on the other end told her that Joe had ended the call.

As she was replaying in her mind the conversation she'd just had with Joe, Tina heard Sean's key in the front door lock. She quickly glanced at her reflection in the glass door of the microwave. Satisfied, she turned and hurried to the door.

"Darling, you're here," she said. "I've missed you so much."

"Not as much as I've missed you," Sean said, drawing her to him. He held her tightly while he glanced at his Submariner Rolex. The men in The Money Club had far more expensive ones, but this watch showed them that he was somewhat in their class. She kissed him deeply, her hands behind his salt and pepper hair, pulling him close, her body molded to his.

She pulled away. "Sean, I bought your favorite wine for you, Archery Summit. Let me get you a glass. I thought we could take our wine in the bedroom and relax." She turned around, then looked over her shoulder, and winked at him suggestively.

"Wish I could, sweetheart, but I'm on a tight schedule. I've just got time for a glass of wine. I couldn't let the day go by without having a chance to at least see you," he said smoothly.

She went into the kitchen and returned a few moments later, holding two glasses of red wine. She handed him one and lowered her eyelids, making them into bedroom eyes. "Are you sure you can't stay a little longer? I'll make it worth your while if you do," she said in a throaty voice.

"Tina, I'm sure you would, but fatherhood calls, in addition to Maddie's demands. Rickie has a dance recital tonight, and it's a must attend thing."

"Good grief, Sean, the kid's only four years old. How big of a deal can it be at that age?"

"Trust me, it's a big deal, both to her and Maddie. She's been practicing for weeks, and it's all Maddie's been talking about."

"Sean, this won't take long, but I need to tell you I'm getting tired of waiting for us to be together. You always have some excuse why you need more time. I want a firm commitment from you. I want you to leave Maddie within the week. If not, it's over between us."

Sean was quiet for a few moments and then he said, "I'm sorry it's come to this Tina. I really thought I could leave Maddie and Rickie, but I can't. I understand what you're saying, and I don't blame you. Just know that a part of me will always be in love with you."

He set his untouched glass of wine down on the coffee table and walked towards the door.

"Sean, if you leave now, I can't be responsible for what happens to you."

"Is that a threat?" he asked, the tone of his voice changing from that of a lover to that of someone who resented being threatened. He turned back towards her.

"My ex-boyfriend called to tell me that if he can't have me, you won't either," she said. *And quite frankly, Sean,* she thought, *if Joe doesn't do something, there's a very good chance I will. In case you missed the memo, men don't leave me. I leave them.*

"So long, Tina," he said as he turned and walked out the door.

As soon as the door closed, she threw herself on the couch in the living room and the first of many tears began coursing down her cheeks as her anger increased moment by moment. She laid on the couch and a wave of bitterness swept over her as she thought about the dire straits she was in. A plan began to form in her mind. Maybe Joe could be of use to her after all.

CHAPTER TWO

Kevin Summers rubbed his eyes and looked again at the numbers on the spreadsheet in front of him. He'd thought he'd been so careful when he'd padded the cost of the items he purchased for use at Casa Flores, but evidently he hadn't been clever enough to outsmart his boss, Sean Holmes. He should have realized anyone who had a Master's Degree from the Harvard Business School might be suspicious when numbers didn't look quite right.

He went over in his mind the meeting he and Sean had earlier that afternoon. It hadn't been pleasant. Sean didn't accuse him of padding the numbers. No, he'd simply said he could tell from looking at the spreadsheet that what Kevin said he'd bought for Casa Flores and what had actually been delivered were entirely different. There was a huge difference. Actually, a difference that amounted to many thousands of dollars.

Kevin had told Sean he didn't know what he was talking about, but his denial fell on deaf ears. He asked Sean if he was accusing him of embezzling money. Sean had replied that he wasn't accusing him, he was simply telling Kevin that he knew Kevin had embezzled money. Anyone with half an eye for accounting could tell the numbers were off.

Then he'd gone on to tell Kevin that he was willing to overlook it on two conditions. First, Kevin would have to repay the misappropriated amount, a sum that Sean had calculated to be $137,250.00, within the week. Second, Kevin would never do anything like that again. Sean said if there was even an iota of evidence he had, or a whisper he had, Sean would call the police and Kevin would not only lose his job, he'd be arrested and probably spend time in prison.

To say Kevin had been shaken to his core by first Sean finding out about it, and second, by what he expected Kevin to do about it, would be the understatement of the year.

There was no point in Kevin trying to bluster his way out of it. Sean had been very cool, calm, and emphatic that he had proof of the embezzlement. Kevin realized he had printed bank statements and merchant delivery sheets spread out on his desk.

Kevin remembered looking at Sean and saying, "Why are you giving me another chance?"

Sean had responded by saying, "The Money Club members like you. You're their main contact at Casa Flores when they come here to stay. With your good looks, the way you dress and act, and the sports information that you always have on hand, they feel that you represent their club well. They would not be happy if they found out about this."

Kevin refrained from saying that the way he dressed, expensively, like the club members, was a result of his embezzlement. He could have told Sean that the reason he was such a font of knowledge regarding sports subjects was due to his addiction to placing large bets on various sporting events. The money he needed to place those bets was also a result of his embezzlement.

His clothing might bring a few dollars at a resale shop. Gambling debts had no value, and he owed over $50,000 to different bookies at the moment. And while he didn't have a degree from Harvard, he was well aware that gambling debts were not an asset.

He knew that an unpaid gambling debt could become very

painful, like the pain from a broken kneecap. He broke out in a cold sweat just thinking about the collection techniques bookies used to collect past due debts.

As far as his looks – well, good genes had helped somewhat, and since this was a town with a plastic surgeon on nearly every corner, it wasn't too hard to enhance the parts that nature had overlooked. A good haircut allowed him to have that Southern California surfer look and hours spent with a physical trainer helped. But he couldn't get back any of that money either.

Now he had to figure out how he was going to get the money he owed The Money Club and the money he owed his bookies, but the prospects of either were seemingly slim or none, and slim had just left the room.

What Sean had said about the club members liking him was positive. Maybe they liked him enough to promote him to Sean's position if something happened to Sean in the future.

He realized that kind of thinking was taking him nowhere. There would be no future if he couldn't return the money he owed the club and his bookies. He told himself that if bets were taken on whether he'd be able to survive being the assistant manager of Casa Flores, which was owned and operated by the members of The Money Club, given his present predicament, the odds would be 1,000 to 1 against him.

Unbidden, the thought again occurred to him that if something happened to Sean, he would be next in line for the job of manager of Casa Flores. If something happened to Sean, no one would ever need to know about the embezzlement. And if something happened to Sean and Kevin got promoted, the salary increase would probably take care of his gambling debts over a period of rime, assuming he could work out a payment plan.

After a few more minutes, the jury in his mind had met and decided that Sean had to be eliminated. That was the only way Kevin could survive this fiasco. He'd underestimated Sean.

CHAPTER THREE

Marty looked at her reflection in the front window of Carl's antique store to make sure she looked okay. She pushed a couple of auburn tendrils that had escaped her chignon back in place, taking note that her multi-colored tan and green blouse accentuated her hazel eyes.

Pleased she'd pass Carl's nonverbal attractiveness rating, she walked into the shop and was immediately greeted by Carl himself. He walked over to her, and in true Hollywood fashion, air-kissed both of her cheeks. "It's so good to see you, darling. You look fabulous! And wasn't that fantastic news about Miles Reed?

"I wrote him back after I got his note thanking me for the Elvis jacket and told him I was thinking about going to Las Vegas to see his show, because I thought he was so fabulous when I'd seen him here in Palm Springs. And guess what?" Carl said excitedly.

"What?" Marty said. *Between the "darling," the "air-kiss," and the "fabulous," I think he's already entered the entertainment world,* she thought.

"He wrote me back and said he'd be honored to have me come to Las Vegas. He even said to let him know the date, and he'd make sure I had a front row center seat, and that he'd leave a ticket for me at the box office. How fab is that?"

"Fab, Carl, really fab. So, to change the subject, what did you want to tell me about the appraisal at Casa Flores?"

"Let's go into my office. We can have a cup of coffee while I tell you about it."

Carl closed the door to his office, walked over to the credenza, and poured a cup of coffee for each of them. "If I remember correctly, Marty, you drink yours black. Right?"

"Yes, thank you," she said, taking the cup from him.

He sat down at his desk, pushed his horn-rimmed glasses up, put his elbows on the desk, and templed his hands in church steeple fashion.

"You look awfully grim, Carl. Seriously, what's this about?"

"Since I'm the one who recommended you for the appraisal, I want to be sure you go into it armed with some background information. I've found it always helps to know who the players are in a given situation."

"Couldn't agree more, so who are the players at the Casa Flores?"

"First of all, the compound is aptly named. People who see it think that's all there is to it. They think some billionaire owns the compound and pays a lot of money to gardeners to keep everything blooming on the property. In Spanish Casa Flores means the flower house."

"Yes, I remember that from my days of taking Spanish in high school, but I'm gathering from what you're saying there's more to it than some beautiful flowers. Actually, it's not too far from where I live, and although it's gated and impossible to see much, I have seen the colorful flowers that border the street, and that's exactly what I thought it was, just a big mansion with lots of flowers."

"Let me start by describing it to you. The compound is backed up to the hills for security reasons and consists of a large central house with four individual suites in it as well as a state-of-the-art kitchen, a dining room with a table that comfortably seats forty, a room that's set up like a large living room which can comfortably seat forty, as well as multiple bathrooms.

"In addition to the main house, behind it are fifteen casitas, each of which has a kitchenette, a great room, two suites, and a private pool," Carl said.

"It sounds fascinating," Marty said. "From what I could see it looked like there was a large glass-walled house with flowers and climbing vines everywhere."

"Yes, that would be a fair description, but that's only part of it. They didn't want the property to be developed in the traditional Spanish hacienda style, because the members are very individualistic and didn't want to do anything that's like what someone else already has done."

"When I got the call from Jerry Jessup, he told me he was the president of the Casa Flores," Marty said. "I thought maybe it was a think tank or some non-profit organization."

"No, not quite." Carl took a sip of his coffee and said, "Casa Flores is the name of the property owned by a very, very wealthy group of men. Have you ever heard of 'The Money Club?' It's in the paper from time to time, although they try to keep a very low profile about it. The last thing the members want is any publicity."

"I may have read something about it, but I don't recall exactly what it was."

"As I said, the property is owned by The Money Club. As members, they are entitled to use the property whenever they want during the year. Most of them live in Los Angeles and stay at Casa Flores when they come to Palm Springs to play golf.

"For one week every year, and that's coming up in a few weeks, all of the members are expected to come to the compound to attend an annual meeting, engage in some fellowship with the other members and participate in some round table discussions led by guest speakers, very important guest speakers I might add."

"Now I remember where I heard the name," Marty said. "I read an article about several past U.S. presidents speaking to a group of men in the desert. That must be where they spoke."

"It is and was. This year will be no different. Since most of these men are on a first name basis with all the presidents of the last few years, it's kind of like old home week for them. Because of who these men are, multimillionaires, if not billionaires, a lot of huge business deals are also done during that week. If you watch the stock market a few weeks after the week they're all here, the deals will be reflected there."

"How do they handle the security that must be necessary, not only for the ex-presidents, but also for the members, and why only men?"

"Men only because it's in their By-Laws, and I grant you that type of thing is a very grey area, but to my knowledge, no one has challenged it as of yet." Carl said. "As to security, as I said, Casa Flores backs up to the hills. Carefully thought out landscaping with an electronic fence surrounds the rest of the property. There is a code for the gate when the gate isn't manned, and it's the only way in and out of the property. Retired policemen guard the property on a 24/7 basis and also man the golf carts that take the members from the parking lot to the casitas where they stay.

"There are several small casitas for the guards and other help on the far side of the compound grounds. A chef lives on the property and is always available when a member wants food.

"Lastly, there is an assistant manager, think his name is Kevin Summers, who takes care of the day-to-day things, like the members' requests, and doing all the purchasing for Casa Flores. It's very well-run and very, very exclusive."

"It sounds like it. Tell me about the appraisal I'll be doing."

"It will be done for insurance purposes. My understanding is that the members formed the club twenty years ago based on a similar club near the Russian River in Northern California called The Bohemian Club. They built the property from scratch – one of the members had owned the land and gave it to The Money Club in lieu of a fee for joining – and then they started buying antiques, painting and furnishings for it."

"You've sold them a lot of antiques, right?" Marty asked.

"Yes and no. You and I both know that in order to be called an antique, the item must be one hundred years old. I've sold them a lot of things that technically don't qualify as antiques, but are very, very valuable collectibles, such as Native American rugs, art pottery, 20th century California impressionist paintings, and things like that, and yes, a lot of antiques as well. That's what you'll be appraising. There won't be any collections like we often do in private homes, such as cut glass or paperweights."

"Who's in charge of buying the antiques and collectibles for the club?"

"When The Money Club was formed, the first president, a man by the name of Henry Marcell, bought things from me and probably from other dealers as well. When he died, the man who hired you to do the appraisal, Jerry Jessup, became the president and has bought a lot from my shop."

"You're not telling me everything, Carl. What are you leaving out?"

Carl was quiet for a moment and then he said, "Well, Jerry confided in me recently that there is a man by the name of Basil Montgomery who desperately wants to become president of The Money Club. From what Jerry told me, the man is enormously wealthy and no one says no to him, but the members did when Jerry and Basil ran against each other to be president."

"Is the presidency a paid position?"

"No, it's strictly a status thing, and believe me, with the egos these men have, every one of them would like to be president, and all of them probably feel they could do a better job than Jerry."

"I can tell you like Jerry, don't you? Since he buys from you, does he live in Palm Springs?"

"I do like him. He's a straight shooter and trying to keep some of the antics that go on out at Casa Flores out of the press requires the tact of a Buddha or someone like him. Personally, I can't imagine a worse job, but like I said, being the president of The Money Club is about as prestigious as it gets for this type of male," he said with a sniff.

"Glad I can't afford it. I really don't think I'd like the members. And yes, Jerry lives in a huge estate in La Quinta. I've also sold him a lot of things for his own home."

"What about the manager? How does he handle the egos?"

"From what I understand, very well. Name is Sean Holmes and his job is more to look after the big picture. You know, making sure that everything runs smoothly. I believe he leaves the day-to-day interaction with the members to his assistant manager, a fellow by the name of Kevin Summers."

"Anything else I should know going into this?"

"There are a lot of rumors that the manager, Sean Holmes, is having an affair with a woman who was previously the wife of one of the members, Basil Montgomery, the one I told you about who wants Jerry's job."

Carl continued, "Obviously, not a good decision on Sean's part. From what Jerry has told me, having an affair with another man's wife who is in the club, even if it's an ex-wife, is simply not done. The last I heard Jerry was going to talk to Sean and tell him it would be a good idea if he broke off the affair."

"Is that a subtle threat that he might lose his job if he doesn't?"

"Possibly. Jerry might feel he has to do that in order to hold on to his position as president. He said he had it on pretty good authority that Basil still wants to be president of the club."

"Well, from what you've just told me, it looks like I may be walking into a can of worms. Thanking you earlier for referring me for this appraisal may have been a bit premature. Think you were smart to stay out of this one."

If Marty had been psychic like her sister, Laura, she might have heard a little voice saying, "You've got it wrong, Marty, you're the one who should have stayed out of it."

CHAPTER FOUR

When Marty got home, the residents of the compound were sitting around the large table in the middle of the courtyard. Her sister, Laura, Les, a very in-demand artist and her sister's significant other, Jeff, Marty's police detective husband, John, the owner of the Red Pony Food Trucks and Catering Company, and his assistant, Max, were sharing the events of their day, as they usually did.

"I'll be joining you in a minute," Marty said. "I want to change clothes and walk the dogs first."

"I just got back from walking them," Jeff said, "so you can scratch that off your to-do list."

She looked at him for a moment, thinking back to when he'd first walked into the house where she was conducting an appraisal. Every instinct in her told her that she'd been waiting for him her whole life. When she married the big, handsome, detective, she'd known her instincts had been right, and she'd said a silent thank you prayer for him every day since.

"Thanks," she said as she went inside their small but cozy home. A few moments later she walked out towards the table. As soon as he saw Marty walking out of her house, John, the resident chef, poured her a glass of wine. When she sat down, he handed it to her.

John Anderson, a very accomplished chef, was the owner of the Red Pony Food Trucks and Catering Company. One of the perks of living at the compound was that every night, unless John had a catering event, he used the compound residents as guinea pigs for dishes he wanted to use for the Red Pony or catering.

His long-time assistant, Max, usually shared dinner with them. Max had lived in the high desert his entire life and was a confirmed, by his own words, "redneck." He was happiest when he was in his truck with his three dogs and his guns. But he was also very good at cooking and idolized his boss, John.

"Thanks," Marty said as she pushed her hair back from her face. "Question for you. Have any of you heard of a group called The Money Club or Casa Flores?"

"I have," Les said. "Two of their members have bought paintings from me. I remember when the first man bought a painting he told me a friend of his, who was in The Money Club, would probably be interested in my work and buy one. He was, he did, and they both paid top dollar."

Marty wasn't surprised to hear that members of The Money Club had purchased paintings from him. Les had developed an international reputation as one of the finest contemporary artists in the United States. Bearded, with a long gray ponytail, he was the epitome of everyone's mental picture of what an artist should look like. He and Laura had been significant others for as long as Marty could remember.

"Were the paintings you sold them for their own homes or for Casa Flores?"

"They were for their own homes. Actually, the gallery that represents me in Los Angeles sold the first one my painting. When the gallery manager mentioned to him that I lived in Palm Springs, he asked if he could meet me the next time he came here. That's all I know about it."

"What did you think of the man you met with?" Marty asked.

Les was quiet for a moment and then he said, "He looked like and talked like a man who had more money than he'd ever need. The painting he bought was one of my most expensive pieces. Usually gallery clients will try to get the gallery to reduce the price on art pieces. I remember the gallery manager telling me it was the first time since she'd worked at the gallery that someone had paid the list price and never asked if the gallery could do better."

"I know from working with antiques and art that doesn't happen very often," Marty said. "Buying antiques and art is often kind of a game for some people. You know, to see how much they can get the price down. What was he like personally?"

"I'm not very sophisticated about clothes, watches, shoes, and things like that, but I do know what a Rolex is, and I was curious after I met with him what the one on his wrist was. When I got back here, I looked it up on Dr. Google. It was a Rolex Platinum Diamond Pearlmaster and goes for about a quarter of a million dollars."

"Good grief," Laura said. "That would sure feed a lot of hungry people."

"I got the impression helping other people was the farthest thing from this man's mind. In the half hour we spent having a cup of coffee, he mentioned the seven homes he had all over the world, his private plane, his three wives, who had all been models, and I've mercifully forgotten everything else. Why do you ask?"

"I've been hired to do an appraisal of some of the personal property of The Money Club. They own the Casa Flores. You've probably seen it when you drive down to Palm Springs. It's tucked back against the hills on the right-hand side of the road just before you get to Palm Springs."

"Oh, I remember it now," John said. "I had a catering event there a couple of years ago. They were hosting a couple of business tycoons. Think it was Bill Gates and Steve Jobs. Anyway, Max and I prepared about ten kinds of really fancy appetizers.

"Security was very tight, and we were instructed to deliver them to the gate where someone would meet us. They would then be transferred to a couple of those long golf carts and taken to their kitchen. I was told their chef would take care of heating them, arranging them, and serving them."

"Which means you never actually went on the property itself, right?" Marty asked.

"No. I asked why security was so tight, and the guy who was driving the cart said Gates and Jobs were expected in a couple of hours. They were going to be giving talks to the members and spend the night. That's all I know. The little I did see of the grounds and the buildings were beautiful. I can sure see why someone named it House of Flowers. They were everywhere."

"Marty, I know a little about them," Jeff said. "Over the years they've hired retired policemen to be guards there. I talked to one of our men recently, and he told me that it's a real sweetheart deal. He said all he has to do is patrol the property and make sure no one has tampered with the fences or the guard gate. They have two guards per eight-hour shift.

"He said they go around the property in their golf carts to make sure everything's okay, but he told me there had never been an incident while he'd been employed there, and he said breaking into the compound would be like breaking into Fort Knox. Wasn't going to happen."

"Thanks, all, and that's pretty much the opinion I got from Carl, you know my friend who owns Ye Olde Antique Shoppe in Palm Springs," Marty said. "But he also told me a couple of other things about the members and the place. Kind of like scratching the underbelly. Anyway, let me tell you what he told me, and then I'd like to hear your feedback."

She spent the next few minutes recounting her conversation with Carl, then she sat back and said, "Well? Thoughts?"

"Marty, I wouldn't worry. Sounds like it's a pretty routine appraisal. And from my perspective, I like it that there's a lot of security around. You'll be fine, but I sure will be interested to hear about it," Jeff said.

It was quiet for a moment, then Laura spoke, "Marty, remember when I told you this afternoon to take Patron with you? I don't think you need to do it, and Jeff," she said turning to face him. "Hate to tell you, but the whatevers are giving me strong signals that it will be anything but a routine appraisal and you'll be involved."

"Swell, that's just swell," Marty said, a perplexed look on her face.

"On that note, my friends, time for Max and me to bring you dinner," John said as he and Max stood up and walked towards John's kitchen. They returned a few minutes later.

"Tonight, my friends, we have a gourmet mac and cheese with a tri-color slaw, garlic bread, and the easiest cake recipe I've ever made that makes my mouth water just thinking about it."

He and Max made several trips into John's house getting more food and when they were all seated, Jeff raised his glass and said, "Please join me in a toast to John and Max. John, your dinners are always the highlight of my day, and I'm pretty sure I speak for everyone at the table."

"*Mangia, mangia*, eat, eat, as the Italians would urge you," John said. "Nothing worse than cold food, although I have been known to have cold mac and cheese for breakfast, and I'll bet I'm not the only one," he said with a wink. From the smiles he saw as he looked around the table, it was very apparent he'd nailed one of their secret vices.

CHAPTER FIVE

"Mr. Montgomery, I'd like to speak to you. I think this is as good as time as any, since no one is around," Mickey O'Dooley, Basil Montgomery's bodyguard said. They were sitting in the back seat of Basil's Rolls Royce limousine on their way to his Malibu estate.

"Certainly, Mickey, what is it?" Basil asked as he glanced up to make sure the partition which separated his driver from the back seat was closed.

"It's a bit of a delicate subject, but I just received a phone call from one of the security men at Casa Flores. He told me that the manager, Sean Holmes, was having an affair with your ex-wife, Tina. I thought you'd probably want to know about it."

"I sure do," he said angrily. "Tell me what you know, everything."

"I asked him how long it had been going on and how he'd heard about it. He told me he'd overheard a telephone conversation between Sean and a woman he kept calling Tina. He thought it was a little strange, because he knew your ex-wife's name was Tina."

Mickey was quiet and Basil realized he was struggling with whether or not he should tell him something. Basil didn't want to push him and remained silent.

After a few moments Mickey continued, "The security man is an ex-policeman from Palm Springs. He called a friend of his who is still on the force and asked him to get information on Tina, and he did."

"And?" Basil asked.

"He got her address and started driving by her home when he was off duty. He saw Sean's car there on a number of different occasions. He put two and two together and made the inference that there was something going on between them." He was quiet again.

"Go ahead, Mickey. I can tell you're debating how much you should tell me. It might help you if I told you that I really don't care what Tina does, but this might prove to be very interesting for me in another way."

"He wanted to be very sure about the affair before he told me," Mickey said, "and he knew the information would be passed on to you ultimately, so he put a wiretap on her phone. Even though it was illegal, he knew it wasn't going to be used in a court of law. He simply wanted confirmation of what he highly suspected."

"Did he get it?"

"He more then got it. From everything he heard, it was very apparent they were having an affair."

"Does anyone else know about it?" Basil asked. "Any of the club members?"

"He didn't say anything about the members, but I did ask him about the president, Jerry Jessup." He saw Basil's face darken at the mention of Jessup's name and well-remembered the bitterness that stemmed from when Basil and Jerry both ran for president of The Money Club, with Jerry being successful.

"My contact said he has a feeling Jerry knows about it, but he couldn't be sure."

"So, you're essentially telling me that the president of The Money Club probably knows that his hand-picked manager of the club is having an affair with the ex-wife of a member, a violation of an unwritten by-law."

"Yes, sir. I thought you'd want to know."

"You did the right thing, Mickey, this is something I definitely needed to know. Thank you."

They were both quiet as the driver pulled off of Pacific Coast Highway and onto a short road just north of Malibu. He clicked open the gates and proceeded up the long driveway that led to the mansion on the hill which had a view of Los Angeles on one side and the Pacific Ocean on the other.

As wealthy as Basil was and as many beautiful houses as he owned throughout the world, this was the one he called home. It never failed to enchant him. On one side of the property were the stables where he raised his prize-winning thoroughbreds, and on the other side, his boutique vineyard (some called them "backyard vineyards" because of their size).

His "backyard vineyard" cabernet sauvignon wines had taken home at least one blue ribbon from each event he'd entered them in and there was a waiting list each year for the new releases. He didn't even have to advertise them, they were so highly prized.

Basil's money had come from his grandfather via a trust fund. His family was considered to be one of the Boston Brahmins, commonly used to refer to the most important families in Boston, most of whom could trace their American ancestry from the Mayflower and 1620.

His grandfather had always told him their family was special. No one could just decide to become a Boston Brahmin. If you weren't born into a Brahmin family, you had to marry into one, and there were a lot of rules about behavior, dress, and speech.

Basil had known that Tina could never be a Boston Brahmin. He regarded her more as a starter wife, thus the prenuptial agreement. When he was ready to settle down and raise a family, he'd marry a woman from one of the East Coast Establishment families. It was preordained, and he'd been told that was the type of woman he would marry for as long as he could remember. It was very important to his family.

What wasn't pre-ordained was losing the presidency of The Money Club. Boston Brahmins did not lose. Period. End of sentence. That's why there was still bad blood between Jerry Jessup and Basil Montgomery. Basil had never told his family that he'd run for president of The Money Club and lost. They only knew he was a member of a very prestigious club in the Southern California area. They would definitely not approve of the loss he'd suffered.

Nor had he ever told them about Tina. They definitely would not have approved of her. Quite simply, she didn't meet the criteria of the Boston Brahmins. Which was exactly why she'd been a starter bride, a one-year wonder.

Once he was inside his estate, he walked over to the bank of windows in the kitchen, looking out at his vineyard, and below that, the Pacific Ocean. Based on what Mickey had just told him, he began to see a glimmer of a chance that he could become president of The Money Club.

If something was to happen to Sean as a result of a seamy affair that the president of the club had known about, but chosen not to do anything about, it would only be fitting to call for an election. Certainly, a president who was indirectly responsible for the negative publicity the club would receive, should not be allowed to hold the office of president.

He stood looking out the windows for a long time devising a plan that would insure his presidency. When he was finished, he turned and called out, "Mickey, please come in here."

Within seconds Mickey was there. Actually, he was never far from

Basil. "Mickey, let's take a walk in the vineyards. I have a little job I'd like you to take care of, and I'd rather not know the details. I think it's better that way."

CHAPTER SIX

"Mrs. Holmes, it's Ryder Tait. I have some information for you," the voice on the end of the phone said. "Would you like me to mail it to you or would you like to meet me?"

"I'd like to meet with you. Do you have anywhere in mind?" she asked.

"There's a Starbucks on the 111 Highway in Palm Desert. Can you meet me there?"

"Yes, I know where it is. What's a good time for you?" she asked.

"The sooner the better. It's noon now. How about 12:30?"

"That would be perfect. I have to pick up my daughter from nursery school at 2:00. See you then."

A half hour later Maddie was seated at a small table in the back of Starbucks, a venti in front of her. The door opened and she saw Ryder, the private investigator she'd hired to find out if Sean was having an affair, which she highly suspected.

Ryder acknowledged her with a grin and walked over to the counter to place his order. A few moments later he joined her at her table. "Good to see you again, Mrs. Holmes."

"Thanks, Ryder. I guess I'll know how good in a few minutes. What have you found out?"

He reached into his briefcase and pulled out a file with her name on it. He shuffled a few papers and took out a manila envelope. "It was just as you suspected. Here are some photographs I was able to get. I think they speak for themselves."

Maddie looked at the intimate photos of the man she'd been married to for ten years and the red-haired woman in disbelief. She looked up at Ryder and asked, "How did you get these?"

"Mrs. Jessup, I'm a private investigator. I never told you that the way I obtain information for my clients would be strictly legal. The only thing I told you was that I would obtain the information you asked me to get. I think these photos show that I did."

Maddie thought she was going to throw up. She'd been hoping against hope that her fears were unfounded, and just a figment of her imagination, but the photos left no doubt that her instincts had been spot on.

"Thank you, Ryder. Obviously, I wish you had come up with other information, because this is going to cause me to make some very painful decisions I never thought I'd have to make. How much do I owe you?"

"Nothing. The retainer you initially paid me took care of everything." He was quiet for a moment and then he said, "I'm really sorry, but it is what it is. If you ask me, with a wife like you, I think your husband is crazy."

"Thanks. Ryder, let me ask you something. Since you don't always follow the letter of the law, how open are you to doing things that might be a little more illegal, perhaps even criminal?"

He was quiet for several minutes and then he said, "Mrs. Holmes, everyone has their price. Why don't you think about what you're willing to pay and call me? You have my number."

Ryder picked his briefcase and coffee cup, smiled at her, turned around, and walked out the door.

I hope she calls and asks me to get rid of him. She's attractive, she obviously has money, and she'll be real lonesome when he's gone. For what he did to her, I'd probably do it for free even if she doesn't call. I could do a lot worse than her, and think how grateful she'll be for what I'm going to do.

Maddie sat at the Starbucks' table for a long time trying to figure out how she was going to pick up the pieces of her shattered world. She had no idea how she could ever face Sean again, because every time she looked at him, she would see him and the redhead in the photographs. They were going through her mind in a continuous loop.

She looked at her watch and saw that she had twenty minutes until she needed to leave to pick up Rickie. She took her phone out of her purse, scrolled through her contacts and found Ryder's number. Then she put her phone down, frightened by the call she'd almost made.

CHAPTER SEVEN

Marty awoke to the smell of coffee, and looked at the empty space on the bed next to her. She decided Jeff must have left for his conference a little earlier than he was planning. She put on a robe and walked into the kitchen, lured by the coffee aroma.

She found a note on the counter from Jeff that read "Morning, sleepyhead. I programmed the coffee, and I'm assuming that's what drew you to the kitchen. The dogs have been fed and walked. Ease into your morning and good luck on your appraisal. I'll be back from the conference before you know it. Love you."

Marty smiled and greeted Duke and Patron. "Morning, guys. Duke, Patron, I spoke with Les last night, and he'll be around today to take you out when you need to go. Other than that, you just can sleep and relax until I get back."

She opened the door that led into the courtyard and took her coffee and iPad with her. Laura was dressed for work, sitting at the table, reading her emails.

"Good morning, Laura. Have a good night's sleep?" she asked cheerily.

"Not particularly, due to you," Laura replied, with a frown on her face.

"What are you talking about?"

"The whatevers were busy last night. I kept seeing you with flowers everywhere, and there was a lot of swirling energy around you."

"All right. I've done this dance enough to know you were getting something from somewhere. Any idea what it all means?"

"Not at this point. I think the flowers refer to Casa Flores, the place where you're going to do the appraisal today. As far as the swirling energy, I take that to mean that there will be a lot going on there, far more than an appraisal."

"Well, I hate to ask this, but based on past experiences, do you see any bodies, you know, like someone's been murdered?"

"No, I don't, but that doesn't mean much. The swirling energy worries me because it usually indicates unstableness, and I really don't like you going into places with that kind of energy."

"Yeah, but you told me I didn't need to have my trusty dog with me today. That should count for something."

"As calm as Patron is being at the moment, even though we're talking about swirling energy, I don't think you're going to be in any danger at all, but I do think you'll be encountering a difficult situation."

"Well, in that case, I suppose I should thank God for small favors."

"Yep, that would be my assessment. I've got to go. After Dick was nice enough to give me the day off yesterday, I don't think he'd be happy if his assistant showed up late today. Something akin to biting the hand that feeds you and all that."

She stood up, threw a kiss to Marty, and walked into her house. A moment later she walked out of it, opened the gate, got in her car, and headed for Palm Springs.

Marty looked at the time on her iPad and realized she needed to quickly shower and dress if she was going to be on time to meet Jerry Jessup at the Casa Flores. Given everything she'd learned about it, and from what Laura had just said, she knew this was going to be an interesting appraisal.

An hour later she put her camera and the other things she'd need for the appraisal in the trunk of her car. She returned to her house, made sure Patron and Duke had plenty of water, gave them a treat, and then left for her meeting with Jerry Jessup.

CHAPTER EIGHT

When Marty pulled into the Casa Flores driveway, she saw a Mercedes Benz sedan in front of the gate. A large man with grey hair and a tan got out of the car and walked back to where Marty was stopped.

"Hi, I'm Jerry Jessup. You must be Marty Morgan. I waited for you, because only members and some of the employees who work here are allowed access to the gate code when the guard's not on duty. I'm sorry, but we do have rules here, and that one is strictly enforced. Just follow me to the parking lot, and one of the security detail will take us up to the main house."

A few minutes later she pulled in next to Jerry's car in the large parking lot, opened the car's trunk, and took out her appraising equipment. When Jerry had gotten out of his car, she said, "I didn't bring my dog with me this morning, but I very well might in the next day or so. My husband's a detective with the Palm Springs Police Department, and he really prefers it if I take Patron with me on my appraisals.

"Since I often appraise things worth thousands of dollars, he feels better knowing Patron is with me. Patron's very well-trained and I promise, he won't be a bother at all."

"Not a problem. A number of our members bring their dogs with

37

them when they come here, so he'll probably find some smells he likes. Ah, there's Jim. He's one of our security guards, and he'll take us to the main house where Sean will be waiting for us.

"Sean's the manager of Casa Flores, and I told him when I spoke with him yesterday that I want him to give you a tour of the house, so you can decide what needs to be appraised and what doesn't. I have to talk to some of the staff while you're doing that, but first I'll introduce you to Sean."

Jerry helped Marty carry her equipment into the house. "These buildings were built for us about fifteen years ago and the architect used a compound he'd seen in Architectural Digest as his prototype. No matter how many times I come here, I'm still captivated by the beauty of the buildings here at Casa Flores. And I feel the same way about the flowers."

"You must have a large landscaping staff, because this is like being in an arboretum," Marty said. "The grounds are simply beautiful." She looked around the house at the glass walls, the cantilevered levels, and the black wrought iron handrail that was formed in the shape of various kinds of flowers. It was stunning.

"I'd differ with you on one point. I used to say the same thing, but recently I was told that a true arboretum is a place where plants are cultivated for scientific and educational purposes. The ones here have no purpose other than to please the members, and from what I hear, they do, so technically this isn't an arboretum."

"Well, whatever, the effect is a visual delight," Marty said.

"Thanks. Follow me. Sean has a very nice office in the rear of the house. Being in the back of the house, if a number of the members are here and talking, he can still work uninterrupted. It even has a sliding glass door that leads outside to the garden area which he usually leaves open on warm pleasant days like today." Jerry walked down the tiled hallway and they passed by a number of doors leading to the rooms Carl had described to her.

Jerry stopped at a door and knocked. When there was no response, he knocked again. He turned to Marty and said, "Maybe he's in the bathroom and can't hear us. Why don't we go in and wait for him to come back."

He opened the door, paused, and then rushed into the room. Marty followed him and saw a man, who she presumed was Sean Holmes, slumped over his desk with a knife sticking out of his back. The sliding glass door behind him was open and a soft breeze was gently blowing the curtains on the door.

"Call 9-1-1," Jerry yelled as he ran over to Sean. A moment later he said, "He's got a pulse. Maybe it's not too late. I'll text security and tell them to open the gates for the ambulance."

Marty made the call, told the operator where they were, and that an ambulance was needed immediately. Moments later they heard the sound of sirens and soon paramedics, firemen, and policemen were filling the room. The paramedics carefully removed the knife, put Sean on a gurney, and rushed him to the hospital.

One of the men walked over to Jerry and Marty, who were standing out of the way at the far end of the room, and said, "I'm Detective Collins. Tell me what happened."

Jerry spoke up and said, "I will, but you can't let the press get ahold of this. Call the hospital and tell them the same thing. I can't have this on the news or in the papers."

"Sir, that's pretty much out of my hands. Between the paramedics, the firemen, the police, and the hospital personnel, I can almost guarantee you that it's going to get out. Why do you have a problem with that?"

"This is one of the most exclusive clubs in the world, and the members are paranoid about their names being leaked to the press or even the hint of negative publicity, which this would be. Please do everything you can so that doesn't happen."

"Well, Mr..."

"The name's Jessup, Jerry Jessup. I'm the manager of the club."

"Well, Mr. Jessup, I'll see what I can do, but there are already a lot of moving parts who have seen a man here with a knife stuck in his back, which, in my experience, means that someone tried to murder the man. I can't guarantee you anything."

"The members are some of the wealthiest and most powerful men in Southern California. Do whatever you can to make it happen," Jessup said.

"When I get back to the station, I'll talk to the chief, but that's the best I can do."

"Considering how much money I, and a lot of the other members of this club, gave the chief in his last campaign, I'll be calling him as well," Jerry said.

"All right, Sir, do what you feel you have to do. My main concern is how this man ended up with a knife in his back." He glanced at Marty and said, "I'll need your statement as well." He turned on a recorder, motioned to one of his deputies to join him, looked at Jerry and said, "Please begin by telling me how you came to be here and what you saw when you entered the room."

Jerry related his movements from the time he'd met Marty at the gate to the discovery of Sean's body. When he was finished, the detective turned to Marty and said, "Please tell me what your involvement is in this as well as how you discovered the body."

Marty told the detective almost the same thing that Jerry had with the difference being that she was there to do an appraisal of items in the building.

"I'm afraid that will have to be put on hold for the present time, Mrs. Combs. This building, actually the whole property, is now an active crime scene. We won't be finished up here for a couple of days. Thank you both for your cooperation, and if we need anything else from you, we'll be in touch. Please give my deputy your contact information. I need to tell my men a few things, so you'll have to excuse me."

Jerry and Marty walked outside and Jerry texted one of the security detail to pick them up and take them to their cars. When they were in the golf cart, the driver asked, "What's going on? I saw the ambulance leave and now the place is crawling with police. Something going down here?"

"No," Jerry said blandly. "It seems Sean had a heart attack, and we didn't want to waste a minute making sure that he got the best and fastest care possible. I'm sure he'll be back here in a week or so."

Marty looked at Jerry and couldn't believe what she'd just heard. At that moment she knew that Jerry and everyone else connected with The Money Club were going to do their best to cover up the attempted murder of Sean Holmes. She wondered if it was going to extend to the police.

CHAPTER NINE

On the drive back to the compound, Marty was torn as to whether or not she should call Carl and tell him what had happened at Casa Flores. She knew he'd be calling her to find out what she thought of the appraisal and the property. However, if she told Carl, within a few hours word of the attempted murder would be all over the Palm Spring area, given the fact that he was well-known as perhaps the biggest gossip in Palm Springs.

She considered Carl to be a very good friend, but she was well aware that a lot of the people who went to Carl's shop went there as much for the gossip as for the antiques. He probably knew more than anyone else in the area about the secrets of the rich and glamorous of Palm Springs. Things they wished would rather never see the light of day.

The more she thought about it, the more she decided that she owed him an explanation of what had happened. After all, he was the one who'd referred her to Jerry Jessup. If she didn't tell him what had happened or whitewashed it, and he found out what had really happened, which, knowing Carl, was a distinct possibility, it would ruin their friendship.

Marty felt she owed far more to Carl than she did to Jerry Jessup. She had been on an appraisal or at least starting one, and she had a firm policy of not discussing what her clients owned or what their things were worth. But in this case, the appraisal had never been started, and Carl already knew who the client was, what most of the items were, and even what they were worth. She decided she needed to talk to him in person.

She drove into Palm Springs and was able to find a parking place in front of Carl's shop, a rarity in the downtown area. She parked and opened the door to his shop.

"Hi, Marty," Carl's assistant, Danica, Said. "Is Carl expecting you? He didn't mention it to me."

"Good late morning, Danica. No, he's not expecting me. I just decided to drop by. Is he around?"

"He went out to get an early sandwich for us. He should be back any minute. Do you want to look around or do you want to go in his office and wait for him?"

"I think I'll go in his office. As I recall, he usually has a pot of coffee going in there, and I could use a cup. When he returns, would you tell him I'm here?"

"Will do. Make yourself comfortable. He's got a lot of magazines and auction reports in there you can enjoy while you're waiting for him."

"Thanks," Marty said as she walked into the office. A few minutes later the office door opened and he said, "Marty, I was really surprised when Danica told me you were here. I thought you were starting the Casa Flores appraisal today."

He sat down at his desk and said, "I hope you don't mind if I eat in front of you, but I'm expecting a couple of big clients in a little while, and I need some sustenance. Now, tell me everything."

"I will, Carl, but first I need a firm commitment from you that what I'm about to tell you will go no further, and I'm very serious about this, deadly so. If it does, you could lose a very lucrative client,

Jerry Jessup."

"That's about the strangest preamble I've ever heard. Okay, you've got my full attention, and I promise not to breathe a word of it, no matter how juicy it is, and how much it may kill me."

"That's not quite the word I'd use given what I'm going to tell you, but here goes." Marty spent the next half hour relating the events of the morning to Carl.

When she told him about Sean being slumped over his desk with a knife in his back, Carl audibly gasped and said, "Oh my God, now I know why I wasn't supposed to do that appraisal. I would have died, just curled up and died if I'd been the one to discover him. Ten toes up. I faint at the very thought of blood, much less seeing it."

"In that case, you definitely would not have done well."

"What did the police say about it?"

"Not much." She went on to tell him about Jerry's request that it not be made public and the detective's response.

"Fat chance of that happening," Carl said. "This town is a cesspool of gossip. Believe me, I should know. When the society mavens get ahold of this, the upper echelons of Palm Spring will be in a feeding frenzy."

"That might be so," Marty said, "but aren't some of those society mavens' husbands members of The Money Club?"

"Yes, about five of them are from the Palm Springs area. The rest are from Southern California, primarily the Los Angeles area, although a couple of them are from Newport Beach. The Palm Springs wives will probably be quiet about it, but I don't think I mentioned that it's almost impossible to become a member of that club. Literally, someone has to die to create a spot for someone to join.

"Trust me on this. If the women whose husbands can't join the club get wind of this, it will be the biggest topic around. What did the police say about suspects or possible motives?"

"Nothing."

"The reason I ask is that, based on the conversation we had yesterday, seems like there might be a couple of people who might have a motive for wanting to kill Sean. I wonder if Sean knew who tried to kill him?"

"I have no idea. Jeff left early this morning for a conference in Los Angeles. I thought I'd call him a little later and see if he's heard anything. I did think it was interesting that there was nothing on the radio about it. I switched to several different stations on my way here, and not a word."

"Marty, how do you want me to handle Jerry if he calls and asks if we talked?"

"I think you should be honest, Carl. Tell him I personally came here to let you know what had happened since you were the one who referred me, and that you consider it to be a confidence, one that won't be repeated. That should suffice."

"One more question and then my clients should be here. How has Patron acted lately?"

"Good question, and I really hadn't thought about it until now. He was nervous when Laura and I first discussed the subject, but since then he's been calm. Even this morning when I left."

"Don't you find that a little odd, based on what we've seen from him before?"

Marty was quiet for a moment and then she said, "Laura has a theory that he only gets riled up, you know growling and barking, if he perceives that there's a threat to me. My take would be that he didn't feel that I was going to be threatened in any way today, and fortunately, I wasn't."

"Well, I suppose that's the silver lining in this. Would you do me a favor and call me after you talk to Jeff? If the police department is going to try and quash this thing, I'd think they'd have to let their head detective know, even if he is out of town."

"Yes, I'll call you after I talk to him."

There was a knock on the door and then Danica opened it and said, "Carl, Mr. and Mrs. Richards are here."

"Thanks, Danica. Tell them I'll be right out." He stood up and said, "Marty, duty calls. Sorry my referral turned out to be not only traumatic, but non-money generating at this point. Let me know what Jeff says."

"Will do, Carl. Good luck with your clients," Marty said as Carl opened the door for her and she walked across the shop to the front door and then to her car.

CHAPTER TEN

When Marty got back to the compound, she saw Patron and Duke waiting for her at their usual place by the gate. She walked over to it and let them out to have a short romp in the desert. They spent the next twenty minutes enjoying their freedom, chasing lizards, and generally having a good time.

"Okay, guys. You've had your fun. Time to go inside."

The three of them walked through the gate and into the courtyard which was empty. Marty looked at her watch and knew that in about an hour and a half the compound residents would be gathered at the large table in the courtyard sharing the events of their day, but for now, all was quiet.

She went into her house followed by Patron and Duke who immediately headed over to their oversized dog beds and laid down. Marty knew they'd be there until it was time for their dinner, which was fine with her. She needed to change clothes and call Jeff. Ten minutes later, comfortable in a pair of jeans and a t-shirt, she sat down at her desk, pulled favorites up on her cell phone, and clicked on Jeff's name.

She was afraid it was going to go to his voicemail, but at the last minute she heard his voice, "Marty, is everything okay? I got a call a little while ago from the chief and sounds like you were at the wrong place at the wrong time. Tell me about it. I'm walking out of the conference room and into the hall now, so no need to hurry."

"I will, and then I'll be very interested to hear what your chief had to say about it." She told him everything, from the time she'd met Jerry at the Casa Flores gate, to when she'd left Carl's antique shop.

When she was finished, Jeff was quiet, which was unusual for him.

"Jeff, I'm very interested in not only what the chief had to say but also your thoughts on all of this."

"Marty, you're probably not going to like what I have to say. It's going to go against that Midwest sense of truthfulness, honor, and justice that's so permanently ingrained in you, but here's what happened. The chief called about an hour ago and told me what had happened. He also told me that you and a man named Jerry Jessup were the ones who discovered the attempted murder. Is that true?"

"Yes, that's just what I told you."

"Well, here's the part you're not going to like. The chief said that since the doctors told him that the victim would make a full recovery, he saw no reason to waste manpower trying to find out who did it. As a matter of fact, in his words, the case is closed."

"Jeff, you can't be serious," Marty said angrily. "That's horrible, a total and complete travesty of justice. What if the person who attempted to murder Sean tries again? I can't believe what I'm hearing."

"Marty, I knew it wouldn't make you happy. I'm just the messenger here. Don't shoot me."

"Why would he possibly make that decision?"

"Sweetheart, at times your naiveté is charming, but this time you're playing with the big boys."

"What do you mean?"

"Unfortunately, it's how the big boys do business. The chief of police is elected. Elections cost money. Several members of The Money Club are big contributors. Are you beginning to connect the dots here?"

"So you're saying that when people who contribute heavily to elect someone, and that someone has the power to quash something, it will be done if they request it? Is that what I'm hearing?"

"Yes, Marty, that's exactly what I'm saying, and that's exactly what is happening with Sean Holmes. Given what I've just been told, I am not to investigate anything, nor will the police department, but I think you should see what you can find out. And there's something else you should know."

"What's that?"

"One of The Money Club members owns the hospital where Sean is and two of the members own the newspapers and news stations in the Palm Springs area. That pretty much guarantees the story won't get much play anywhere other than on some obscure radio station, and if it's questioned, the response will be something like 'if it was legitimate, it would have been on the well-known stations.' Are you getting the picture?"

It was Marty's turn to be quiet. "Yes. Jeff, remember everything I told you last night, you know, what Carl told me. Several of those people would certainly have motives and could be considered suspects. I wonder if Sean has any idea who did it?"

"The chief told me that there was a guard assigned to Sean. In other words, he sits outside Sean's room to make sure nobody from the press or anyone else gets in to see Sean. The chief shared that because several of the men who work as security guards at Casa Flores were in my department.

"I'd bet everything that their loyalty is to me, rather than the chief.

If you're agreeable, I'll make a couple of calls, and if you happen to go to the hospital tomorrow, I would imagine you could get into Sean's room and talk to him. I'll talk to whoever is assigned to guard Sean's room."

"The chief said he was sure Sean would make a full recovery, and that he was doing very well. That would make me assume he'd be able to talk to you tomorrow. What do you think?"

"I think if Jerry Jessup ever finds out I'm doing this, he'll find another appraiser."

"Marty, this is your decision, and I don't want to sway you one way or the other. Why don't you think about it and get back to me? I'll hold off making any phone calls until I hear from you. I have to get back to a meeting. I ducked out just to take your call, and I've been gone long enough."

"Jeff, wait a minute. I've made my decision. Make your calls and then let me know if it will work out. Tell whoever's on guard that I'll plan on being at the hospital about 9:30 tomorrow morning. The doctors and the routine morning things should be done by then."

"That was a tough decision, Marty, but one I don't think you'll ever regret. And I'm sure Sean will think you made the right decision. Love you and talk to you later," he said as he ended the call.

Marty put her phone down on her desk and decided not to call Carl. She really didn't want him to know about her involvement in this. She could always say she got busy and didn't have time to call him.

CHAPTER ELEVEN

When Marty got off the phone with Jeff, she realized the enormity of what she was undertaking. If The Money Club members were really that influential, and if they ever found out that she was actively involved in a case that the police chief had officially closed, the members could very easily make sure that she never had another important appraisal in the Palm Springs area (read that, large fee appraisal). Essentially, her career and the business she'd worked so hard to build would be finished.

She thought long and hard about whether or not she was doing the right thing, and then she remembered something her mother had always told her when she was a little girl – if you do it, will you be able to sleep at night? – and conversely – if you don't do it, will you able to sleep at night? The situation always dictated which of those phrases her mother would use.

When Marty thought about it in that way, she really had no choice. If she didn't attempt to find out who tried to murder Sean Holmes, she wouldn't be able to sleep at night. If she did nothing, her appraisal business might still be a success, but she'd have to judge herself a failure as a human being. Ultimately, it became a no-brainer.

She heard sounds coming from the courtyard and realized that the evening ritual was starting to take place. The residents of the little four-house compound had become not only her best friends, but just as much a family to her as Laura was. She fed the dogs and went out to the courtyard.

"How was the appraisal?" Laura asked. "See or have anything happen that was of interest?"

"Yes. It was more than interesting and unusual."

"What do you mean?" John asked. "I thought this was to be a pretty straightforward appraisal, just one that was taking place at some fancy schmancy location."

"I really need to talk about this and get your input, but I'm going to have to ask something of all of you, and if you can't agree to it, I'll understand."

"What are you talking about?" Les asked.

"I need each of you, Laura, Les, John, and Max, to never repeat anything I'm about to say. I need to have a strong confirmation from each of you."

The group was quiet for several moments, sensing that something quite unusual was going on. Marty had never asked that of them before. One by one, each of them agreed.

"Marty," John said, "before you get started, I think we're going to need a little sustenance while we listen to you. I'm going to make a little appetizer plate for us. Don't start until I get back." He returned a few minutes later with a charcuterie platter – different kinds of meat, cheese, crackers, and nuts.

"Okay, dish, girl, dish. We're all waitin' fer ya'," Max said.

Marty recounted the events of the morning, as well as her conversations with Carl and Jeff. "I have to tell you this was the hardest decision I think I've ever had to make," she said.

"And I know what made you finally decide," Laura said. "The

words Mom always said to us - if you do it, will you able to sleep at night? – and conversely – if you don't do it, will you able to sleep at night? Would I be right?"

"Yes, that's exactly what finally swayed me. I just hope that Jeff has a good retirement plan with the police department, because my sources of income may be taking a serious hit in the near future."

"No, they won't," Laura said. "You don't need to worry. What you do need to do is go over all of the possible suspects with this man named Sean. Tell him that you've been told the police intend to close the case. He knows the men in this club, and I'm sure he'd be the first to understand the need for a blackout on this."

"That's good advice, Laura. Anything else?"

"Yes, he must be concerned that whoever tried to kill him might try again. If no one investigates the crime or finds out who did it, that person will be free to try again. That's bound to concern him. I'd use that ploy to get as much information out of him about the possible suspects as you can."

"What should I tell Jerry Jessup?" Marty asked.

"Why do you need to tell him anything?" Les asked. "Your relationship with him hinges strictly on the appraisal. I think I'd call him in a couple of days and ask what's going on at Casa Flores. Then you can inquire about the status of the appraisal. He doesn't need to know anything about your relationship with Sean."

"Something that will be interesting to see is how this is going to affect Jerry Jessup and Basil Montgomery's relationship. Jerry's going to be all for the blackout on the attempted murder so the other members don't find out, but if Basil still wants to be president, he's going to want some explanation of what happened to Sean and see if he can pin his absence on Jerry," Laura said.

She continued, "I don't know what the relationship is, but I know it's all tied up in the attempted murder. See what you find out. Once in a while my vibes are wrong."

"Haven't seen it yet in my lifetime," Marty said. She turned to John, "I'm exhausted and hungry. What's for dinner tonight? Enough of this heavy stuff."

"Barbecued swordfish steaks with garlic butter, spinach salad with bacon dressing, and for dessert, drum roll please, a berry pudding with a macadamia caramel sauce."

"I have just two things to say to that," Les said. "First, be still my heart, and second, bring it on."

Later, after the group was sated and kudos had been given to John and Max for another incredible meal, Laura said, "Marty, you don't need to take Patron with you when you go to the hospital tomorrow, mainly because you don't want to attract attention, but I have some thoughts on this."

"Okay, shoot."

"Sean definitely holds the key to a number of things. He could be pivotal in the power play between Basil and Jerry. And don't forget about his affair. I'd look into the woman he's having an affair with. I'll bet Jeff could get someone to do a check on her and see what comes up. Try that."

"May I tell him you said that?" Marty asked.

"Sure, but why?"

"Because he has a great deal of respect for your whatevers. Simple as that, and on that note, dear friends, I'm off to bed."

"Tell you what, Marty," Les said. "Jeff's off attending some conference in Los Angeles and you've had a rough day. I'll walk the dogs. The desert always gives me inspiration, and I had a couple of hours today of what writers would call 'writer's block,' only I call it 'painter's block.' I'm sure it will be over tomorrow. Leave your door cracked open, and I'll let them in and then lock it."

"Thanks, Les. See you all tomorrow."

CHAPTER TWELVE

The next morning Marty was up early. She walked the dogs, fed them, and then sat down at the kitchen table with a notepad, pen, and a cup of coffee. She began her research by making a list of the suspects and everything she knew about them which, admittedly, wasn't much.

Then she made a list of the suspects' relationship to Sean and possible motives. A lot of it was conjecture, but when she was finished, she had Basil Montgomery and Tina Quinn. She added Sean's wife for no other reason than she may have known about the affair.

Marty read through her notes and realized she didn't have much to go on and without help from the police department and Jeff, this was going to be far more difficult than usual. She looked at the time and decided Jeff should be up by now and that his meetings wouldn't have started yet. She pressed Favorites on her cell phone and clicked on him.

He answered on the second ring. "Good morning, sweetheart. I hope your bed was as cold as mine was last night. I missed you."

"I missed you too, but I was so tired, I definitely slept. Jeff, can you call someone and see what you can find out about a woman named Tina Quinn? I heard from Carl that she's the woman who was having an affair with Sean. Other than Basil Montgomery, those are the only suspects I can come up with. Slim pickings, at best. Maybe Sean's wife could be considered a suspect, but I have nothing to base that on other than she might have known about his affair. More may come after I talk to him, but for now, that's it."

"Consider it done. You know, Marty, a man like Basil Montgomery would never dirty his hands and do something like murder someone. He'd pay someone to do it for him. I'm going to run a check on him as well. By the way, Sean's room number is 415.

"I got it from my deputy who has the duty there this morning. Don't check in with the receptionist on the ground floor. The chief told the owner of the hospital to alert the reception staff that no one is to be allowed in Sean's room. The less anyone knows what you're doing, the better.

"Since you're going to do this, might as well get all the information you can about the players. I should have something for you later today. Call me after you talk to Sean. He may be able to give you another name or two. I wish I was there with you. Aside from the crime, the foibles of the rich and powerful are always interesting."

*****

Later that morning, Marty walked into the hospital, went past the reception desk, and took the elevator to the 4th floor. When she got off, she looked down the hall and saw Jeff's deputy sitting in a chair next to a closed door. She took her driver's license out of her wallet and walked towards him.

"Hi, I'm Marty Morgan, Jeff Combs' wife. Here's my identification. I'd like to talk to Sean for a few minutes. I also have heard how boring doing something like this can be, so I brought you some brownies. Enjoy."

She didn't tell him she'd made them several weeks ago and pulled them out of the freezer right before she'd left her house. Having at least one law enforcement person on her side was a good start to the investigation.

"No problem. Detective Combs called and told me to expect you. He even gave me your description. The doctor's been here, Sean's eaten breakfast, and several nurses have been in and out doing things like giving him a sponge bath. Think they're probably through for a while, so you picked a good time to come."

He stood up and opened the door for her. "Thanks," Marty said. She walked over to the bed where Sean was laying and said, "Good morning, I'm Marty Morgan, Detective Combs' wife. How are you feeling? You certainly look better than when I saw you yesterday. I, along with Jerry Jessup, were the ones who discovered that someone had tried to murder you."

"My back hurts, but the doctor says that's to be expected. He told me I was very lucky that the knife wound was shallow. He said he assumed that whoever did it was interrupted, which is a good thing.

"I'm waiting for the police to come, so I can give them the names of some people who might have done it. Actually, I'm rather surprised they haven't been here yet."

"Sean, there's something you need to know. I have it on good authority that The Money Club does not want your attempted murder made public. They don't want the publicity. As I understand it, the chief of police, the hospital, and some of the press venues are owned by their members. To put it bluntly, your case has been closed."

Sean looked at her and struggled to get up on one elbow. Marty could see from the pain in his eyes the effort it took. "You're kidding me, right? Someone tried to murder me, and they aren't going to investigate it? Is that what you're telling me?" He lowered himself back on the bed. "I don't believe this."

"Yes, that's exactly what I'm saying. Sean, several times in the course of conducting appraisals I've been involved in solving murders, and fortunately, I've been pretty successful. From time to time I've also helped my husband, who's the lead detective with the Palm Springs Police Department, with his cases. I feel a personal connection to the case since, as I told you, Jerry Jessup and I were the ones who discovered you. Quite simply, I'd like to help find out who tried to murder you."

"You really don't think the police are going to get involved in my attempted murder?" he asked.

"That's right. I believe that's a very bad decision on their part, but I've been told the decision was made purely for political reasons. In order to help you, I'm going to need your cooperation and help. Would you like me to try?" Marty asked.

"Considering that my options are rather limited at this point, yes. Where should we start?"

"Well, I suppose the first question that I should ask you is did you see the person who attacked you?" Marty asked.

"No, I was sitting at my desk when the attack happened. My assailant must have snuck into my office through the open sliding glass door behind my desk. I didn't see anything. I just suddenly felt a sharp searing pain in my back and then I passed out. The next thing I remember is when I woke up in the hospital."

"Sean, I'm sorry, but I need to ask you about your relationship with a woman named Tina Quinn. I was told that you were having an affair with her."

"How did you find that out?" he asked in astonishment.

"It doesn't matter. What's important now is that you tell me about it."

He took a sip of the water from the glass that was on the table next to his bed and said, "Yes, I was having an affair with her, and note that I used the word 'was' in describing it. About a week ago she gave me an ultimatum – that I either leave my wife so Tina and I could be together - or our affair was at an end. I told her it was time to end it. She threatened me. I think the words she used were 'I can't be responsible for what happens to you' and then she said something about her ex-boyfriend."

"Do you know his name or anything about him?"

"No, not much. Early in our relationship she said something about being glad I didn't have a criminal record, because she was finished with men like that."

"Does that mean you think her ex-boyfriend has a criminal record?"

"I don't know, but based on what she said, I would think he might."

"Sean, I was told that Tina had been married to Basil Montgomery, one of The Money Club members. Is that true?"

"Yes, although I didn't find out she'd been married to him until several months after our affair had begun."

"How did you find out?"

"Not from her. Several of the club members were in the large living room one evening, having drinks and talking. The door to my office was open, and I could tell they were talking about their ex-wives. Mr. Montgomery was talking about the fact that he'd had a starter wife for a year, but he got rid of her because his family would never approve of her, and that they expected him to marry a woman from the East Coast establishment.

"He said he wanted to find out what marriage was all about before he married for real. Someone asked him if she lived in Southern California and he said, and I think he'd had too much to drink, 'Yes, the very beautiful red-headed woman, my ex-wife whose name is Tina Quinn, lives right here in Palm Springs.

CHAPTER THIRTEEN

"All right," Marty said. "I'll definitely look into Tina. Tell me what you know about Basil."

"He's from one of the founding families of Boston. Believe me, he wants everyone to know that, and he considers himself to be above everyone else because of it. As all the men in the club are, he's very wealthy. I believe his money comes from a trust fund his grandfather set up for him."

"Does he work, or just live off the money from the trust fund?" Marty asked.

"He raises thoroughbreds. From what I've heard he's had a couple of them do well in very important races. I know he uses those as stud horses. He also has a boutique winery that produces prize-winning cabernet sauvignon."

"Are either of those things profitable?"

"I would think the horses are. Sometimes I go down to Del Mar, you know the race track near San Diego, and I see his name in the horse racing papers, and many a time he's had several horses in the races down there. As far as the winery, I doubt it. Very few of those are commercial successes. It's more a hobby for people who have some extra money, actually a lot of money, because it's a bottomless money pit. I'd think his winery would fit into that category, but I could be wrong."

"Thanks, Sean. I don't know how any of that information can help us find who tried to murder you, but I like to get a total picture of anyone I might consider to be a suspect. What about people around him, you know, gatekeepers? As wealthy as he appears to be, I'd imagine he'd have a few."

"He has a bodyguard by the name of Mickey. The bodyguards and gatekeepers of the members are not allowed in the main house for the dinners and meetings, but they usually sleep in the casitas on Murphy beds that are there for just that purpose."

"Well, if Basil did it, or had it done, since I rather doubt he'd want to personally get his hands dirty, Mickey might be worth taking a look at. What's his last name?"

"I don't know. Now that I think about it, I'm not sure I've ever heard it," Sean said.

"I'll see if it comes up when I run a check on Basil."

"You might ask Jerry Jessup. He could probably tell you. I kind of remember that all of the bodyguards have to have a security check run on them before they're allowed on the property. Jerry must have the information on that because even though I'm the manager, I don't have it."

"Yes, he probably could, but if I asked him, he'd wonder why, and then we've got a problem with me looking into it. I'll be honest with you, Sean. What I'm doing could cost me my career."

"What are you talking about?" he asked.

"I'm an antique and art appraiser. People who have antiques and art usually have a lot of money. Those people are the type of people who would be in The Money Club or their friends would be. If someone found out I was helping you and the word got out among the wealthy in Palm Springs, my career could be over."

"Yes, I see what you mean, even though you'd be doing it for the right reasons."

"That's true," Marty said. "But the very wealthy and you and I often consider the right reasons to be different things. In their mind, a right reason to do something would involve not looking into a crime that would reflect negatively on their club."

She sat back, wondering, as she verbalized it, if indeed, what she was doing was very smart, and if she would have been better off to have left it alone. But as she wondered about it, she knew she couldn't do otherwise and live with herself.

"Sean, how did your wife take this?"

He was very quiet and couldn't meet her eyes.

"Sean, I don't mean to pry, but I need to know everything I can if I'm going to be able to help you."

He looked back at her and said, "I don't know if she's aware of it."

"You're kidding! Surely the police would have called her."

Marty began to put two and two together and then she said, "And I'm guessing that you haven't called her either. Would I be right?"

"Yes."

"Sean, if I'm going to be able to help you, I need to know everything about any altercation you've had with anyone, any problems with anything, and whatever else you can tell me that might shed some light on this situation. Please, tell me what's going on with you and your wife."

CHAPTER FOURTEEN

Sean remained quiet for several long moments and Marty could tell she'd struck a nerve by bringing up his wife.

"Sean, this is just a wild guess, but did something happen between you and your wife as it relates to Tina?" she asked.

He sighed deeply and said, "Yes. This is very hard for me to talk about, so please bear with me. About a week ago I ended the relationship with Tina and went home because my daughter, Rickie, was going to be in a dance recital. When I got home my clothes were all in the courtyard in the front of our home. Our house has an adobe wall in front of it which forms a courtyard. The neighbors couldn't see the clothes, but I sure could."

"What did you do?"

"The gate was locked, but fortunately I had my key. I walked into the courtyard and there was a note safety-pinned to my clothes," Sean said in a halting voice.

"Sean," Marty said softly, "what did the note say?"

Tears formed in the corners of his eyes and he said, "The note said that Maddie had found out about Tina and was divorcing me. It also said that I would never see Rickie again. She told me not to ever contact her again and that the locks on the house had been changed. She said the next thing she'd hear from me was when her attorney contacted me."

"Oh Sean, I'm so sorry. What did you do?"

"I put my clothes in the trash bags she'd laid out and then I went to a nearby hotel. That's when it got ugly. When I tried to rent a room, I found out that my credit card had been cancelled. I asked them to run two other cards. They, too, had been cancelled.

"I told them there must be some mistake and I'd clear it up in the morning and told the reservation clerk that I could write a check, which I did."

"Let me guess," Marty said, "your account had been closed."

"Exactly. No credit cards and no money. She effectively tied me up in knots. I knew that an attorney could eventually take care of it, or at least get some source of funds for me, but at that moment, I had nothing."

"What did you do?" Marty asked.

"I went to my office at The Money Club and that's where I've been sleeping and eating for the past week."

"Did you try and get in touch with her? Do you want the marriage to end?"

"First of all, yes, I tried her cell phone and the house landline. Both of those numbers were no longer in service. Secondly, did I want the marriage to end? Absolutely not. I love Maddie. I've always loved Maddie. As a matter of fact, her father was the one who got me this job."

"Whoa, this is getting a little involved. Let's go back. How long have you and Maddie been married?"

"Ten years. We got married a couple of years after we graduated from UCLA. I went on to get my Master's at Harvard and since she was from Palm Springs, she came back here and worked for an interior design company that specializes in doing condominiums. If you've been here for any amount of time, you can well imagine that with the large number of them that we have here in the desert area, there's no lack of business."

"Yes, I would agree with you on that. Tell me about her father."

"We got married, and I was trying to decide which accounting firm I wanted to work for. Her father's best friend is Jerry Jessup. Jerry mentioned that he'd just been elected as president of The Money Club and was looking for a general manager, someone who gets along with very wealthy people and who was also very smart. Maddie's father recommended me."

"Let me interrupt you for a minute, Sean. Do you think Jerry has told Maddie's father about what happened to you?"

"No. Jerry and Herb, that's Maddie's father, had a major falling out a couple of years ago about, of all thing, whether or not Maddie's father had cheated on his golf card. Jerry was convinced he had, and that was the end of the relationship."

"Wow, that seems like one of those things where the punishment doesn't fit the crime."

"Yeah, but if you knew these men, you'd see how it could happen. They are two of the most egotistical and stubborn people I've ever known. No one was surprised that they'd rather let a lifelong friendship go than have either one of them admit they were wrong."

"Okay, back to Maddie. What now?"

"I hired an attorney, and I'm hoping when I see her that I can make her understand that Tina was something that simply happened at a vulnerable time in my life. Guess I was one of those classic guys who looks in the mirror one day, sees the salt and pepper in his hair, the lines on the face, and decides a fling will make him young again. It didn't."

"Did you tell Jerry about it?"

"No, I didn't want him getting in touch with Maddie's father and the two of them reconciling on the back of the end of my marriage."

"I can understand that. I hope you realize I'm going to have to look into Maddie's whereabouts the morning the attempt on your life was made."

"Whatever for? Maddie would never hurt me," Sean said his eyes wide.

"Probably not, but she was mad enough to cancel your credit cards and bank account, as well as change the locks and telephone numbers. Jealousy can often be a motive in cases like this."

"I don't think so. Do what you have to do, but I'll never believe that," Sean said firmly.

"Okay, Sean. I have Tina, Tina's ex, Mickey, Basil, and Maddie. Can you think of anyone else?"

He was quiet for several minutes and then he said, "Yes, there is someone else who needs to be looked at. His name is Kevin Summers, the assistant manager of The Money Club."

CHAPTER FIFTEEN

"Okay, Sean, tell me about Kevin Summers," Marty said.

When Sean tried to sit up to drink some water, it was obvious he was in pain.

"Sean, would you like me to call a nurse?"

"No, they'll just want to give me something for the pain, and I'm not a real fan of being drugged. I'll wait until it gets worse, but if you could pour some of that water from the jug into my glass, I'd appreciate it."

"Of course," Marty said as she stood up to help him. When he was finished, she took the glass from him.

"Thanks. For some reason I'm really thirsty."

"I don't know what they've given you, or what's in that IV attached to your arm, but whatever you've had, water is probably the best thing to flush out your body. Let's go back to Kevin Summers."

"All right, and then I think I need some sleep. All of this talking has worn me out, and the doctor said that I need to rest to get back my strength."

"I'll leave right after you tell me about Kevin Summers," Marty assured him.

"Kevin is my assistant manager. I hired him several years ago. I thought he'd be perfect for the job. He'd worked for several nonprofit organizations as a manager. He's a good-looking guy, physically fit, and charming. I thought the members would really like him, and I was right. Kevin is very popular with them."

"I'm not seeing a problem," Marty said.

"Trust me. You will. A problem in the amount of $137,250," Sean said.

"Okay, tell me about it."

"A couple of weeks ago I noticed a difference between the amounts being shown as purchases for The Money Club and the actual bills of lading. The amounts shown on the books were much higher than those. I began investigating and found that over the past year, there was a difference of $137,250. My assistant manager, Kevin, is the one in charge of ordering the supplies for the club."

"Who signed the checks to pay the purchases?" Marty asked.

"Kevin. After he worked for me for two years, I thought it would cut down on my workload to just have him on the checking account rather than me having to sign all of the checks. It made my job a lot easier and saved me a lot of time."

"I'm gathering that didn't go well."

"No. I confronted Kevin about it, probably a week ago, and gave him an ultimatum. I told him I knew he'd been embezzling funds from the club and that he'd be fired unless he returned the money to the club within a week's time. I had all the evidence spread out on my desk, and he knew there was no reason to deny it."

"Sean, why didn't you go to the police about it? That's a very substantial amount. We're not talking about petty theft," Marty said.

"Not in the eyes of the members of the club. They'd take $137,250 as a loss every day of the week to keep the club from having bad publicity, which would have happened if I'd gone to the police. And I knew if I told Jerry about it, he'd tell me not to go to the police.

"Believe me, that amount is a mere pittance to the members. Plus, they really like Kevin. As I said, he's very charming, he's knowledgeable about sports, and he looks like one of them. He's pretty much the face of management to the club members."

"Has he paid back the money he owes?" Marty asked.

"As of yesterday, no."

"What do you think will happen now?"

"I don't know. I assume he's taking over for me in my absence. Whether he'll pay the money back, I don't know."

"Did you tell anyone else about Kevin's embezzlement?"

"No. I'm the only one who knows," he said.

"I hate to say this, but that's a pretty powerful motive for him to attack and try to kill you. If you'd died in the attack, from what you're telling me, there's a good chance he'd be promoted to the position of manager, and not only would the money not have been paid back, he might just continue to embezzle."

"I hadn't put all that together, but you're probably right," Sean said.

"Okay, I've been here long enough and I agree with your doctor. You need your rest. I'll leave you now, but could you give me your cell phone number? I don't think the switchboard will put calls through to your room."

"Sure, my wallet's over there. Take one of my cards out. Marty, one thing's been bothering me since I regained consciousness. Do you think because whoever tried to murder me was unsuccessful, they'll try again?"

"I have no way of knowing, but I think you should be very alert to anything unusual for the next few days. Sean, are you aware that the police have stationed a man outside your door?"

"No, I haven't been out of my room. Why did they do that?"

"I'd like to say they're doing it to stop a murder from happening, but given what we've found out, I think it's more to make sure that no publicity is caused by you being here, like the press not getting wind of this."

He was quiet for a moment and then said, "Well, I suppose I'll just have to take what they give me, and if they're giving me protection, even if for the wrong reason, at least I'm being protected."

"Sean, take care of yourself, and I'll do everything I can to find out who did this. Sleep well," Marty said as she walked over to the door and quietly let herself out. She nodded to the guard sitting by the door who was contentedly munching on one of the brownies she'd given him, walked down the hall, and left the hospital.

CHAPTER SIXTEEN

Marty looked at the dashboard clock on her car and realized it was almost noon. She decided to call Jeff and see if the morning session at his conference had broken for lunch. A moment later she heard, "Glad you called. I was getting worried about you. I called my deputy who's on guard at the hospital a little while ago, and he told me you were still in with Sean. How did it go?"

"I think very well. He seems to trust me. Of course, given that the police department isn't going to do anything to help him, it's not like he has a choice. Here are the main points of what he said."

Marty spent several minutes filling Jeff in on her conversation with Sean. When she was finished, he said, "I think you have a lot of meat there, Marty. Sure, a couple of them jump right out at me, but you can't overlook anyone. Here's what I found out.

"Tina Quinn, as we know, was married to Basil Montgomery for a year. They had signed a prenuptial contract and according to its terms, she got a nice house and $250,000 as a settlement. Not bad, but for someone like Tina, not enough.

"She became involved with an investment broker, Joe Barton, who showed her the good life. Problem was in order to show her the good life he had to play fast and dirty with some of his client's money. One of them called him on it, and he ended up spending several months in prison. He got out for good behavior.

"He recently found employment with an investment company whose owner is very religious and prides himself on, according to the website I saw, believing in man's ability to atone for his sins and giving everyone a second chance. According to the records of his company, it's doing quite well, so that approach must work. Might want to talk to the owner and see where Joe was the morning of the murder."

"Will do. I'll need the name of the company and the address."

"It's in Palm Springs. Here it is," Jeff said as he gave it to her.

"I'm in Palm Springs right now. I think I'll go there and see what I can find out."

"Be careful, Marty. You don't want to alert anyone as to what you're doing."

"I will, promise. Now, tell me more about Tina Quinn."

"Same story you've heard before. She went to Hollywood to become a star because she was the most beautiful young woman in the small town where she was from in South Dakota. The only job she could get while she was making the casting rounds was as a waitress at a restaurant in Malibu.

"One day Basil Montgomery ate there. She was his server. He took her home to his Malibu house, and a few weeks later they were married. He had a home in Palm Springs they'd go to often, and when they were divorced, she got that house.

"She met Joe and then dumped him when he got caught with his hand in the cookie jar. Then she took up with Sean. She's a real sweetheart, but from the picture I saw of her, she's a beauty. I can see why men are attracted to her."

"And if you're smart, you'll tell me that you're not attracted to her," Marty said.

"I'm smart. I'm not attracted to her, and I only have eyes for you."

"That was the right thing to say, Jeff. Now tell me what you found out about Basil."

"Man, is that guy a piece of work," he said as he told her about Basil's home in Malibu, his family, his horses, and his vineyard. "From some of the things I read, the guy has an ego that's beyond oversized. One article I read said he thinks it's his given right, based on his blue blood, to have the best horses, the best wine, the best whatever he wants. The only thing is he already seems to have the best of everything. In a perfect world it wouldn't be fair."

"Okay, I get all of that, but what's troubling me is why he'd bother to marry Tina. First of all, from what we know of him, he believes he's the preeminent blueblood, and marrying her was really marrying beneath his status. Secondly, why didn't he just have her as his mistress? That doesn't make sense."

"Who knows? If I was a betting man, I'd bet she had something on him, and the house, settlement, and the marriage were the payoff for her not going public with it. Be interesting to know what it was."

"Agreed."

"Anything else?"

"Yes, I was able to find out about Basil's bodyguard, Micky O'Dooley. He's big and very, very good at martial arts. I mean he's in the master category. He studied in Asia for several years with the best of the best. He has no prison record, but there's no doubt that he could do a lot of physical damage to people that, with his martial arts training, would be hard to prove. He's worked for Basil for five years, and Basil is rarely seen without him."

"What I'm hearing is that a man like Mickey wouldn't resort to using a knife. If he wanted to do someone in, he could use one of the martial arts he'd mastered. And if that's true, then he probably didn't do it."

"I'd agree with one stipulation, Marty. If you were known to be superb in a martial art that could result in someone's death, then you might want to use a knife to throw people off."

"Yeah, even though it muddies the waters, it makes sense. Okay, I'll go see if I can get an alibi for Joe Barton and at least I can check one of the suspects off. Jeff, I'd like you to see what you can find out about Maddie Holmes, Sean's wife, and the guy who's his assistant manager, Kevin Summers."

"Will do. Okay, I need something to eat to get enough energy to make it through the afternoon session, plus I have to give a presentation at 3:00. I should be through about 4:00, so I'll call you later to see what you've found out. Love you and miss you. Give the dogs a hug for me and tell everyone at the compound hi."

"I'll take care of it. Good luck on your presentation."

"Thanks," Jeff said as he ended the call.

CHAPTER SEVENTEEN

A little later Marty pulled her car into a strip mall parking lot and thought it was a very strange place for an investment company to be located. She checked her address to make sure she hadn't made a mistake. The addresses agreed and then she saw the sign for the company she was looking for, New Investments, at the far end of the building.

She'd thought about the excuse she'd use for calling on the owner of the company and had come up with the idea of pretending to work as a freelance writer and a friend of hers had told her about an investment company who hired people who had been in prison.

Marty opened the door of the company and was pleasantly surprised by the tasteful way the reception area had been decorated. She walked up to the reception desk and said, "Hi, my name is Marty Combs, and I'm a freelance writer. I'm doing an article on companies that hire people who have been in prison, and your company's name was given to me. I was wondering if I might speak to the owner or the manager."

The young receptionist smiled at her and said, "I'm so glad that you're doing that. I wish more people knew about companies like ours. The manager's at lunch, but the owner, Jack Corbin, is here. Let me see if he has time to talk to you." She stood up and walked down the hall.

A few moments later she returned and said, "Mr. Corbin said it would be a pleasure to talk to you. His office is the third door on the left."

"Thank you," Marty said and walked down the hall. She knocked on the door the receptionist had indicated and heard a pleasant male voice say, "Come in."

"Hello, Mr. Corbin, I'm Marty Combs. Thank you for taking the time to talk to me."

"Please, Ms. Combs, have a seat," he said gesturing to a comfortable chair on the other side of his desk which faced him. "Susie told me you're doing an article about companies that hire people who have been in prison. Is that correct?"

"Yes, I was told your investment company does that. Could you tell me a little bit about it?"

"Certainly. I served time in prison and had a conversion experience while I was in there. When I came out, I was a different man than the one who had gone in. I made a vow that I would show people by my actions and becoming a success, that ex-cons could make it in the world without resorting to crime. I accomplished that goal by starting this company which is designed to help ex-cons."

"That's very commendable. I know it's often difficult for people who have served time in prison to find work. Since you own an investment company, I would assume that you look for people who had been in that profession prior to serving time. Would that be correct?"

"Yes. All of the people, the eight I have working for me presently, were sent to prison for committing what are commonly called 'white-collar crimes,' usually some type of fraud that involves money. These crimes are non-violent and usually don't involve a lot of prison time. I can say with pride that none of the people I've hired has ever had a hint of crime attached to their names since."

"Can you give me a thumbnail description of the type of people you hire? Let's say, your most recent hire. Is that doable?" she asked, hoping that it would be Joe Barton because the timing would be about right.

"Sure. His name is Joe Barton, although if you want to use his name, you'll have to get his permission to do so. He committed a white-collar crime, went to jail, and from what he told me when he applied for the job, was afraid he'd never be able to work in this industry again. I prefer to hire people who have committed misdemeanors rather than felonies, simply because of public opinion.

"Joe was one of those. He's not only good with investments, he's a natural with customers. He has an air about him that simply makes you trust him. My only complaint is that he's a workaholic. He's here from five in the morning, getting ready for the markets to open, to eight at night, long after the markets have closed. I've cautioned him about burn-out, but he assures me that he loves what he's doing."

"You mean like this week he'd be keeping those hours?" Marty asked.

"Yes. I happened to get here yesterday morning at 6:30, because one of my clients is very concerned about some of his investments, and I thought I better watch them closely. The market opens at 9:30 on the East Coast, so we get it here at 6:30.

"Sure enough, when I came in, Joe was here, he'd made coffee, and he was ready for the day. It probably was a good thing he was here early yesterday morning, because he had back-to-back clients all day. He never had time to go out for lunch, and I finally asked Susie, our receptionist, to go out and get him a sandwich about 2:00. I figured it was the least I could do."

Well, so much for Joe Barton. That's a pretty powerful alibi, Marty thought.

"That's a wonderful story, Mr. Corbin, and I certainly will use it in my article, if I can sell it. Again, I really appreciate you taking the time to meet with me. I think what you're doing is wonderful, and I wish you and all your employees the best of luck," Marty said as she stood up and walked over to the door.

"Ms. Combs, if you think of any other questions, I'd be happy to answer them. Here's my card. Good luck with the article," he said as he opened the door for her.

As she walked out to her car, she wished Joe the best.

CHAPTER EIGHTEEN

On her drive back to the compound, Marty decided to stop by the Hi-Lo Drugstore and pick up some photographs she'd recently left to have developed there.

She walked in the front door and saw her friend, Lucy, the manager of the photo department talking on the phone. She walked over to the counter and Lucy raised her hand in acknowledgment, indicating she'd just be a few minutes.

While Lucy was on the phone Marty checked her cell phone to see if Jeff had called. Then she looked at the time and realized he was right in the middle of his presentation. She sent a do well text to him, hoping it would help him, not that he needed any. She'd sat in on some of his presentations before, and they were always excellent.

"Well, girlfriend, ya' jes' won't believe what Killer did. That was my ol' man on the phone, and that darlin' dog of ours jes' brought in a lizard from outside. Walked right up to the ol' man and dropped that sucker on his foot, proud as punch. Ol' man says we gots us a huntin' dog and oughtta' get him perfessionally trained."

"Lucy, I don't think having a dog bring in a lizard is quite the same as having him retrieve a duck or something like that."

"I unnerstan' where yer' comin' from. Duke's too sweet to hunt and Patron already knows where all the animals are, so it wouldn't be much sport fer him, bein' psychotic and all."

"Whoa, Lucy, think you mean psychic, not psychotic. Patron is definitely not psychotic," Marty said.

"Ya' jes' never know. Here's what my word of the day was this mornin'. Are ya' ready?"

"Sure, Lucy, lay it on me."

"Okay, girl, here goes. 'Such short little lives our pets have to spend with us, and they spend most of it waiting for us to come home each day.' John Grogan, ya' know the guy who wrote Marley and Me, said that. Have to agree. That Killer can't git enuf' of us when we get home."

"I swear when I go out to get the mail and come back, Killer greets me like I been gone for weeks. Course I gotta say, gets me right in the feels. Know what I'm sayin', girlfriend?"

"Yes, Lucy, I do," Marty said thinking of how Duke and Patron waited by the gate for her and happily greeted her each time she came home.

"Here's them pics you sent last week. Purty, but not as much as some other stuff people let ya' look at. Course I wouldn't throw it outta' my house if I had it."

"Thanks, Lucy. Great service as always. Well, guess I better be going."

"Wait a sec. Any luck findin' out who tried to off the guy at The Money Club?"

Marty was rarely at a loss of words, as she was sure her husband could attest to, but at the moment, quite simply, she was at a loss for words.

"Lucy, what are you talking about?" Marty asked, wondering how she'd found out and how much she knew.

"Aw girlfriend, when ya' gonna realize people jes' talk to me? One of them guards out at that fancy Casa place lives up here. When he came in for his pics, he was purty upset. Said originally he'd been told the dude had a heart attack, but he'd found out that weren't the case. He was a l'il shook up, I'll tell ya' that.

"Can't tell ya' his name, but it looks to me like them rich boys at The Money Club gots themselves problems jes' like everyone else. Kinda' nice to see. Don't worry. I can see it written all over yer' face. Unnerstan' ya' gotta' keep the lid on this one. I was jes' wonderin', that's all."

"Lucy, this is important. For a number of reasons, this has to be kept under wraps. If it isn't, someone, perhaps several people, could get hurt. Please, do me a favor and tell me his name."

"Marty, ya' ever hear the expression 'If I tell ya' I'll have to kill ya?' Well, that's kinda' what's goin' on here. Let's jes' say things ain't always what they seem to be, and ya' ain't the only one who's got interestin' pics.

"Them pics of the guy who almost got offed and his girlfriend...Well, let's jes' say I needed a cold shower after I saw them."

"You saw pictures of the man who was almost murdered and his girlfriend?" Marty asked, clearly astonished.

"Said enuf, I have. Got nothin' more to tell ya'. It must be serengeti 'cuz that guy who took the pics jes' happened to mention to me that the dude was the manager of some mucky-muck club. Jes' added two and two together. Math ain't my best suit, but think it worked here."

"Lucy, the word is serendipitous, not serengeti. That's a desert in Africa."

"Yeah, well, whatever."

Marty knew Lucy well enough to know she wasn't going to get anything more out of her, so she said, "Lucy, if you change your mind, let me know. I'll be back in a few days with some other photos. Give Killer and your old man a hug for me."

"Will do, girlfriend." She turned to the customer who had been patiently waiting behind Marty for nearly five minutes while Lucy had gone on and on. "So, whatcha' need?"

CHAPTER NINETEEN

After leaving the Hi-Lo Drugstore, Marty drove to the nearby compound and was met, as usual, by two very excited dogs waiting at their favorite place for her, by the gate that led to the courtyard.

"Hey Marty, all of us got back here a little early today and we're just waiting for you to start the party. I've got a glass of wine ready for you and figure you could use it. We want to hear everything that's going on," John said. "I'll hold dinner until we hear all the details. By the way, Duke and Patron got antsy a little while ago, so I took them out. Please sit down and join us. No excuses."

"Thanks, John. It's been a frustrating day. The good news is I eliminated one suspect. The bad news is I have several more to go."

"You know, Marty, there's an old saying that goes something like 'things aren't always what they seem.' Might keep it in mind with this case," Laura said.

"Did Lucy call you?" Marty asked.

"Lucy who?"

"Lucy, the manager of the photo department at the Hi-Lo Drugstore."

"No, why would she?" Laura asked.

"Because she said those exact words to me a few minutes ago. Are you two on the same wave length or something?"

"I have no idea, but the whatevers have been telling me that you shouldn't waste your time on the low hanging fruit. Something about looking beyond what people are telling you or what they think."

"Thanks, Laura," Marty said sarcastically. "So what you're essentially telling me is that I'm wasting my time talking to possible suspects."

"No, I feel you have to do this to get to whoever did it. Kind of like at the end of a rainbow, there will be a pot of gold."

"Or in this case a would-be murderer."

"And that, too," Laura said.

"Okay, ladies, enough," Les said. "Marty, please tell us about your meeting with the victim and what else you did today."

"It was interesting. I have some new suspects to look into," she said, casting a dirty look at her sister, "who may have had something to do with it or might be able to give me some additional information. Here's a recap of my day, and by the way, Jeff says to tell all of you hi."

She spent the next half hour telling them about her conversation with Sean, her meeting with Jack Corbin, and her most recent encounter with Lucy.

"That's pretty much where I'm at now. Tomorrow I plan on talking to Sean's wife, Maddie, and his ex-girlfriend, Tina. I'd like to talk to Basil and his bodyguard, but since he lives in Malibu, I'll have to think about how I can do that. Plus, it would probably be very difficult to even get a meeting with him. I'd bet he's got a whole bunch of gatekeepers in addition to his bodyguard."

"I wouldn't worry about it," Laura said enigmatically.

"Is that from you or the whatevers?" Marty asked.

"Can't tell. It's just a feeling I have," Laura said.

"Well, in that case I'll put some credence in it. The whatevers are rarely wrong, and if you're feeling something, that's probably where it's coming from."

"Okay everybody, tonight it's just leftovers from the Red Pony's food truck. I had a bunch of potato salad, baked beans, and brownies I had to bring back here, so thought I'd barbecue some burgers and make it really simple tonight. Hope that's okay with you."

"Are you kidding?" Les asked. "Your leftovers are better eats than what most people eat when company's coming to dinner. Bring it on."

CHAPTER TWENTY

After dinner was finished and the compound residents had headed off to their respective homes, Marty took the dogs out for one last walk of the day. Even though she hadn't done much physically during the day, she was still exhausted. When she went into her house, she realized she'd left her phone there during her walk, and she'd missed a call from Jeff.

She returned his call and a moment later heard his cheerful voice, "Marty, I was wondering where you were. Figured some dark, handsome stranger had asked you out to dinner on the pretext of having you appraise something for him. Kind of similar to that old line, 'Wanna come up to my place and see my etchings?' Remember it?"

"No, I don't. Is that something you made up?"

"No, it's from my favorite author, Raymond Chandler. His character, Philip Marlowe, was always saying it. He wrote in the 30's and 40's."

"Jeff, I know you're older than I am, but that was waaaayyyy before my time. And I was out in the desert with two dogs rather than with a tall, dark, handsome stranger. How did your presentation go?"

"Well, but it's always nice to have it over with. I don't care how many you give, there's always a little nag that something will go wrong, like your laptop will go on the fritz, so you can't give your Power Point presentation, or you have a senior moment that lasts an hour. You know, the litany of the what ifs."

"Fortunately, you're the one who has to do those presentations on a regular basis. I don't."

"Were you able to get into the investments company?"

"Yes, and I crossed Joe Barton off the list. Here's why," she said telling him about her meeting with Jack Corbin, the owner of the investment company.

"Agreed, but there's still a few others."

"There are and tomorrow I want to try and talk to Tina Quinn and Sean's wife, Maddie. By the way, I had a weird experience with Lucy at the Hi-Lo today."

"I've never had an experience with Lucy that was anything other than weird," Jeff said. "What's the latest?"

"She knew about Sean. She wouldn't tell me exactly how she knew. It had something to do with a guard at Casa Flores as well as a guy who'd taken some pictures of Sean and I guess, Tina. She said they were really something."

Jeff was quiet for a long moment and then said, "Marty, it sounds to me like the work of a private investigator. They always try to get compromising photos of the person they're being hired to investigate. When you talk to Sean's wife tomorrow, ask her if she hired a private investigator. As for Lucy. I'd bet the PI had the photos developed by her. If he lives around where we do, I think that's the only place you can get photos developed. It's quite an interesting coincidence, but certainly within the realm of possibility."

"I will. And I guess I don't need to ask Tina about her ex-boyfriend, considering what I found out earlier today."

"Agreed, but don't discount her. Spurned lovers have certainly been known to commit murder. Have you thought of an excuse you can use for talking to Basil? He certainly has the motive to do it."

"No, I haven't, and quite frankly he's pretty high on my list. I'd like to find out more about him from Jerry Jessup, but if I ask Jerry anything, he'll wonder why, and his loyalty is to the club and keeping this whole thing from going public."

"True. Well, as creative as you are, I'm sure you'll come up with something. I'm meeting a couple of the other detectives in the lounge in a few minutes to discuss some of the new technology we heard about today. It sounds good, but I'm not sure how it can be implemented, and I want to pick their brains."

"Enjoy and sleep well. I'll talk to you tomorrow. I'm off to bed. Loves!"

"Loves and sweet dreams."

Marty had just turned off the light on her nightstand when her phone rang. She looked at the bedside clock and saw it was 9:30. It was late, but not so late that she needed to panic about a call coming in at that time of night.

She picked up her phone and saw that the caller was Carl. "Good evening, Carl. You caught me just before I was going to drift off to sleep. What's up?"

"Marty, I've been bothered by our conversation yesterday, particularly about Basil Montgomery. I realize he has a double motive for getting rid of Sean, one, because he was having an affair with Basil's ex-wife, and secondly, because if he could discredit Jerry, he would probably be able to force a new election and would stand a good chance to win."

"Yes, we're definitely on the same wavelength regarding Basil."

"But here's where I was having a problem, Marty. I couldn't see Basil getting his hands dirty. Yes, he could have had his bodyguard do it, but it still would lead back to him. The way he's always telling people about his family being first generation Bostonians, I couldn't see him taking a chance on besmirching the family name."

"Two things, Carl. First, if he didn't want to besmirch the family name, why did he marry Tina? I can't believe he was able to keep that a secret from his family. Additionally, you used the past tense regarding your concerns about him. That makes me think you've found something out about him."

"I can't answer the first one, but yes, I have found something out, and I think I can save you a lot of trouble."

"Carl, I'm wide awake now. Shoot."

"Okay. Remember how I told you about that celebrity website that I subscribe to?"

"Yes."

"Well, the celebrities aren't just movie stars and people like that. They also keep up-to-date on the activities of the very, very wealthy, like in Basil Montgomery wealthy."

"I'll take it from what you're saying that you went to the site and requested information on him."

"I did. I found out that he and his bodyguard, the report specifically mentioned him, because it said Basil never travels anywhere without him, have been in Boston for the last week visiting Basil's family. From that, I think you can cross him off of your suspect list."

Marty was quiet for a few minutes. "Are you absolutely certain of that, Carl?"

"Yes, and I'm emailing the report to you. Basil and his bodyguard,

Mickey, are expected to return to Los Angeles tomorrow morning. Unless he hired someone else, which is possible but unlikely, he didn't have anything to do with it. I'm not saying he won't benefit from it, but I think his hands are clean."

"And taking it one step further. If he isn't, and he did hire someone to do it, it would be like looking for a needle in a haystack. I rather doubt I could ever find out who did it."

"Agreed. Are you planning on talking to Basil's ex-wife?"

"Yes, I'm hoping to do that tomorrow. Why?" Marty asked.

"It still bothers me why he married her. He's lived a very conservative and conventional life. Marrying her seems to be quite inconsistent with everything else about him."

"I've thought the same. I'll see what I can find out and get back to you. Thanks, Carl, I really appreciate this. I was wondering how I'd ever get a meeting with him, but now it looks like I don't need to."

"You're welcome. Just keep me in the loop. You know, inquiring minds…"

"Well aware of it, Carl, and I know how inquiring yours is. Thanks again," she said as she ended the call.

I could have told him about my meeting today and Lucy, but knowing his inclination to gossip, I think I'll tell him as little as possible until I know more, Marty thought as she drifted off to sleep.

CHAPTER TWENTY-ONE

The next morning, after calling Sean and filling him in on the events of the previous day, Marty decided to just go to Tina's home without calling first. She was afraid Tina wouldn't agree to see her and thought the element of surprise might work in her favor.

She fed and walked the dogs, then texted Les asking him to walk them if he had chance. He usually stayed up late working on his current painting and they had an agreement that she should text him if she wanted him to walk the dogs, rather than knock on his door or call, possibly waking him up.

On her way into Palm Springs she looked through the grilled gate at Casa Flores to see if there was any activity, but all she saw were vibrant flowers. It was clear to her that the police chief was as good as his word. The case had been closed, and no one was there investigating the attempted murder of Sean Holmes.

She easily drove to Tina's home following the directions on her GPS. It was a beautiful Spanish Revival style home in the Palos Verdes Estates not far from Palm Canyon Drive.

Marty parked her car in the circular driveway and walked up the driveway to the door which was flanked by floor to ceiling frosted glass panes. She could see some movement inside the house, but she couldn't tell what it was. She rang the doorbell.

A few moments later the door was opened by a beautiful red-haired woman with the greenest eyes Marty had ever seen. As green as her eyes were, Marty wondered if she accented them with colored contact lens.

"Yes," the woman said.

"Hi, my name is Marty Combs. I'm looking for Tina Quinn. I'd like to talk to her for a few minutes. Would you be her?"

"Yes, I am. May I ask what this is regarding?"

"It's regarding the attempted murder of Sean Holmes."

Tina gasped and stood in the doorway staring at Marty. Finally, she said, "Come in. I've not seen anything on the news about this."

Marty followed her into the charming mid-century home and her appraiser's eye couldn't help but admire the way the home had been decorated. Comfortable, stylish, and not the least bit pretentious.

"Is Sean all right?" Tina asked as she motioned for Marty to sit down.

"Yes, he is. Evidently whoever tried to murder him was thwarted, so other than being rather uncomfortable, he's expected to make a full recovery."

"What is your involvement in this?"

"I'm working with a private investigator. Because of Mr. Holmes' relationship with The Money Club, not only is there a news blackout on the attempted murder, the police have also closed the case. Naturally, Mr. Holmes is quite concerned about his safety, afraid that whoever tried to kill him, will try again."

"And why are you here and what do you want from me?" Tina asked.

"Quite frankly, it was well known that you and Mr. Holmes had a relationship that went on for several months. Because of your closeness with him, I'm hoping you might know something that would help us find his would-be murderer."

Tina was quiet for several moments, then she said, "I haven't seen Sean or talked to him for over a week. We ended our relationship on a bitter note. I rather doubt I can help you."

"Ms. Quinn, we also know that you were married to Basil Montgomery, one of the members of The Money Club. Is that correct?"

"Yes, but I fail to see what that has to do with Sean."

"Since Sean is the manager of The Money Club, it might be important. I've been told that there's bad blood between the man who hired Sean, Jerry Jessup, and Basil. Do you know anything about that?"

"Not much. I know that Basil hates Jessup because they both wanted to be president of the club, but Jerry won. I remember Basil saying that "the Boston Montgomerys don't ever lose." He lost the election a couple of years before we were married, and he was still very bitter about it."

"If you don't mind, Ms. Quinn, I'd like to ask you something rather personal."

"You can ask, but I can't guarantee that I'll answer it. What's the question?"

"Why did Basil Montgomery marry you?"

"That's a rather hurtful question, Marty. I mean you could have said you're so beautiful and charming, I can certainly see why Basil married you."

"That's true, but I'm thinking more of Basil's background, his family. I understand that he's from one of the original families who founded Boston, as he likes to say, a Boston Brahmin, and quite proud of it. From my research on the Boston Brahmins, they only marry within their group of old East Coast families. That makes me wonder why he married you if he was so into family traditions. And I'm also wondering why the marriage was so short-lived."

Tina was quiet for a long time, then she said, "I don't think it has anything to do with Sean's attempted murder. As a matter of fact, I've held this in so long, I really would like to tell someone about it, and telling you is not a violation of my divorce agreement with Basil. I only promised to never divulge it to the press."

"I'm sorry, but you lost me," Marty said. "You never promised to tell what to the press?"

Tina sighed deeply and then said, "Several weeks before Basil and I were married, I found an envelope in his nightstand. He was out in the vineyards with his manager. I was curious and opened it. I wish I never had, because those photographs still haunt me."

"What was in the photographs?" Marty asked.

"They were young Asian girls, very young girls, and Basil in, how shall I put it? Let's just say rather compromising positions."

"What did you do after you discovered them?"

"I cried for the girls. Some of them looked like they were only ten or twelve years old. I cried for being with a man who did things like that to young children. And then I decided that if I had to be involved with someone who was obviously sick, I might as well get what I could out of it."

A tear slid down her cheek, and Marty felt that her pain over the girls' predicament was genuine.

Tina continued, "When Basil returned to the house, I confronted him about the photos. He admitted that it was a hobby of his when he traveled to Thailand. I couldn't believe that sexually abusing young girls was nothing more than a hobby to him."

"I'm having a hard time believing it as well, and I don't even know him," Marty said.

"I told him I was going to tell the press about him unless he married me. He told me he couldn't because of what his family would say about it. We hammered out an agreement. We would stay married for one year. At the end of the year he would give me $250,000 and this house. In return I promised I would not go to the press.

"In all honesty, the marriage was one in name only. He made me sick."

"Did his family ever find out about the marriage?" Marty asked.

"Yes. One night he received a call from his father, a very angry father, wanting to know if there was any truth to what he had read in the paper that morning. Specifically that Basil had married a wanna-be starlet. That's how his father referred to me."

"What happened?" Marty asked.

"Basil lied and told his father that he'd gotten drunk when he was in Las Vegas and didn't remember a thing. The part about Las Vegas was true. We got married in one of those tacky little chapels they have over there. He went on to tell his father that he'd been smart. He'd gotten me to sign a prenup agreement. He told his father he was divorcing me rather soon.

"Basil neglected to mention that there was also an agreement which gave me the house and a cash settlement of $250,000. Rather doubt daddy would have been happy to hear about that."

"Well, considering what you just told me, I think you came out the winner."

"I agree, although looking back, I think I probably could have gotten more. I'll remember that next time," Tina said.

"Next time?"

"Yeah, probably. I started seeing a man from the health club where I work out. He's divorced and about thirty years older than I am. The funds from my divorce settlement are getting a bit low, so maybe it's time for me to get married again."

Wow, Marty thought, *I can't imagine living my life by going from one marital relationship to another and be completely casual about it.*

"Well, I wish you good luck."

"A thought just occurred to me. I really did love Sean, and although I could have personally killed him when he ended our relationship, I don't want any harm to come to him. In between Basil and Sean, I was seeing a man who went to jail. He called me recently, and when I told him I didn't want to see him, he wanted to know why. I told him that I was involved with someone."

"Did you tell him who?" Marty asked.

"No, but if you found out about Sean and me, I'm sure others could as well."

"Is his name Joe Barton?"

"Yes, how did you know?" Tina asked.

"We do a pretty thorough job when we conduct an investigation," Marty said, hoping her little white lie would go unnoticed when she went to meet her Maker.

"What did you find out about him?"

"He has an airtight alibi for the time that Sean's would-be murder took place. You don't need to feel guilty about telling him. He's clear."

"I'm glad. I'd hate to be the person responsible for Sean being hurt. In many ways he was a good guy, just a little too tied to his family."

"Yeah, seems like a lot of men are. Thank you so much for the information you've given me. It helps, and I hope your relationship with this new man in your life works for you."

"Me too. You know the old saying about baby needs new shoes. Well, I'm getting a bit antsy because my Jimmy Choos are beginning to look dated. My mother told me that when I got to Hollywood to remember that a woman is judged by her jewelry and her shoes. I've got all the jewelry I need, but new shoes? Definitely."

Marty stood up and walked over to the door. "Thanks again," she said as she opened it and walked out to her car.

Well, if Tina's mother's words are valid, Marty thought, *I'm in real trouble. I imagine shoes from Walmart and a zirconia tennis bracelet instead of a diamond bracelet wouldn't make her mother's list, or for that matter, Tina's either.*

CHAPTER TWENTY-TWO

Marty drove to a nearby Starbucks and got her favorite, a salted caramel mocha. She looked around, saw an empty table with very few people nearby, and called Sean to tell him about her meeting with Tina.

"She told you that about her marriage to Basil? Wow! I always wondered what that marriage was about. Makes sense now. By the way, I got a call this morning from Jerry Jessup, you know, the president of The Money Club."

"Yes, what did he have to say?"

"He asked about my condition and when I'd be ready to return to work. I told him in about three more days."

"How did he sound?"

"Very concerned about my condition, and very glad that I didn't have any lasting injuries, but here's the interesting part. Remember, I told you about my assistant, Kevin Summers?"

"Yes, of course."

"Well, it looks like he's gone. He didn't report to work the morning I was knifed. I assumed he was just late, but he's never been back since. Jerry called his cell phone, but got a message that it was no longer a working number."

"That is interesting. What do you make of it?"

"Could be one of two things. He could be my would-be murderer. Then again, he may have just left town rather than pay back the money he'd embezzled. I have no way of knowing. And if he left, he wouldn't know about the attempted murder."

"What about his personal life? Is he married? Does he have a family?"

"He has a family somewhere in the Midwest, but I don't know where. He's not married. He much preferred the life of a bachelor, changing his ladies at a whim. I really don't think any of them lasted longer than a couple of months. During the time he worked for me, he talked about a number of different ones."

"Do you know if he belonged to a health club? Seems to me you said he was pretty physically fit. If so, maybe they'd know something," Marty said.

"Let me think for a minute. I believe he did, but I just can't remember the name of it. He lived in La Quinta, so maybe it's in that city. Sorry."

"No, that's okay, Sean. You just continue to heal. I'm going to try and see your wife this afternoon. Have you talked to her?"

He was quiet for several moments and then he said, "No. I've thought about it, but as I told you, she's changed her phone number. I'd like to talk to her. If a divorce is inevitable, I would prefer that it be amicable, particularly for Rickie's sake."

"If I get a chance to see her, I'll relay that message."

"Marty, if you do have a chance to talk with her, please tell her that my affair with Tina was the stupidest thing I've ever done in my life. I'd give everything I have to turn back the clock and replay that part of my life. All I want is to be married to Maddie and be a father to Rickie. I love Maddie. I've always loved Maddie. Please tell her that for me," he said in a tearful voice.

Marty had to steel herself not to cry, just listening to Sean. It brought back memories of several years ago when she'd found out about her ex-husband having an affair with his secretary. Everyone in the small Midwestern town where they lived knew about it. Everyone that is, except Marty.

She still smarted every time she thought about it. As she listened to Sean, she wondered how different her life would have been if her ex-husband had shared Sean's thoughts about the stupidity of his affair. Then Marty decided it was a good thing he hadn't, because she would have missed out on finding the love of her life, Jeff.

Lots of truth in the title of Shakespeare's play, "All's Well That Ends Well" she thought, *even though if someone had told me that at the time, I would have said they were crazy. Glad I listened to Laura and came out here to California. Now I not only have Jeff, I have some wonderful new friends. Yes, it is ending well.*

"I'll give her your message, and I hope it helps. Is there anything else I can do for you?"

"No, I'm feeling stronger, and I think I should be out of here in a day or so."

"Take your time. Your body needs some rest after what it went through. I'll call you later today or tomorrow."

"As a matter of fact, Marty, you could do something for me."

"Sure, what is it?" she asked.

"If you have a chance to talk to Maddie, would you call me and tell me what she said? If there's no chance of a reconciliation, I better start accepting it and figure out how I'm going to live the rest of my life."

"Sean, it's too early to give up hope. Sometimes wounds need a little time to heal, be they physical or emotional. Your physical wounds are healing, maybe Maddie just needs some time for her emotional wounds to heal."

"Yeah, you're probably right."

"I promise I'll call you after I talk to her," Marty said.

"Thanks. I'm listening to my body and right now it's telling me it needs some sleep."

"Well, by all means, get some sleep," she said, ending the call.

CHAPTER TWENTY-THREE

Marty usually put her laptop in its carrying case and brought it with her whenever she went into a Starbucks. She knew they had Wi-Fi there and whenever she was in a Starbucks coffee shop, she always seemed to need to find something on the internet, and it was a lot faster than her phone. Plus, it was a lot easier to read.

Today was no exception. She got it out of its case, booted it up, and began searching for physical fitness gyms located in the La Quinta area. She found a number of them and then spent some time thinking about the best way to approach whoever answered the telephone. She needed a cover story for why she wanted to know if Kevin Summers was a member.

She finally came up with what she thought was a pretty foolproof plan. She'd tell the person that she was a waitress at The Spaghetti Spot and Kevin had just eaten lunch there. She'd tell them that he'd left his credit card at the restaurant, and she was trying to find out if he was a member at the fitness club, because he'd said something about working out at a gym in La Quinta after he finished lunch. She complimented herself on the ingenuity of her plan and began to put it in action.

Five calls later, all of which resulted in the person answering the call saying that they'd never heard of him, she began to doubt the wisdom of her plan. Maybe he worked out closer to where The

Money Club was located. She made a mental note to check out the ones a little farther out of Palm Springs and closer to where she lived. But first, she'd finish up her list of La Quinta fitness clubs.

On her sixth call, she hit pay dirt. "Yes," the person who answered the phone said. "We do have a member by the name of Kevin Summers, although he hasn't been here for the last couple of days."

"I see. Well, would it be possible for me to make an appointment with the manager of the club? I kind of hate to leave a credit card at the front desk. I mean if something happened to it, I could be held responsible since technically, he left it with me at the restaurant."

"Yeah, I get it. Let me check with the manager, Bob. I'll put you on hold and be back in a minute."

"Thanks." She sat there sipping her coffee and listening to the background music on her phone while she waited for the decision on whether or not Bob would be available to see her.

A few minutes later, the person said, "Bob could see you at 3:30 this afternoon, if that would work for you."

"Actually, that would be perfect. My shift ends at 3:00. I'll be there at 3:30, and thank you. See you then."

Marty looked at her laptop and realized she had about two hours until her appointment with Bob at the fitness club. She pulled Maddie's address up on her computer and saw that Maddie's house was only a mile or so from the Starbucks where she was.

She thought she'd have a better chance of Maddie talking to her if she didn't give her time to think of an excuse over the telephone not to talk to her. A face to face attempt would probably have a better chance of success. She packed up her computer, finished her coffee, and walked out the door, hoping that Maddie would talk to her.

She was glad Jeff was out of town, because she didn't think he'd be very happy that she'd met with Tina without Patron, and was planning on meeting with Maddie without Patron by her side, both of whom could be considered prime suspects in the attempted murder of Sean.

Well, she thought, *that's just the way things happened to go today. I'm sure if I was in critical danger, Laura would arrange for the heavens to deposit Patron in my path via some of her whatever ways.*

With that thought in mind, she headed for Maddie's home, hoping to get information from her and a reconciliation for Sean.

CHAPTER TWENTY-FOUR

The Starbucks where Marty had been was fairly close to where Maddie lived. It was an older section of Palm Springs where the homes were set back quite a ways from the curb with large lawns. Marty had always thought having a large lawn that required so much water was ludicrous when one lived in what was technically a desert, but from the number of lawns she saw in the neighborhood, a lot of people disagreed with her.

She parked in front of the medium-sized Mediterranean style home with the standard red tile roof, cream colored adobe siding, and enclosed courtyard. She walked up to the gate and saw that it was unlocked, walked through it, and rang the doorbell.

A moment later a voice said, "Who is it?"

"It's Marty Combs. I'm a friend of Sean's, and I'd like to talk to you."

There was a pause and then the door was opened by a dark-haired woman wearing yoga pants and a t-shirt. Even though she wore no makeup, she was very, very attractive.

It's obvious from seeing Tina and his wife that Sean likes attractive women, Marty thought.

"I'm Sean's wife, Maddie. Come in," she said as she opened the door for Marty. "We can talk in the living room." She walked towards a room that was off of the entryway and gestured for Marty to follow her.

"Please, have a seat. I don't have much time to talk, because I need to pick up my daughter at her nursery school, in a few minutes. What can I help you with?"

"Mrs. Holmes, I hate to be the bearer of bad news, but your husband was the victim of an attempted murder. However, I want to assure you that he's all right."

A number of emotions passed across Maddie's face and then she said, "I haven't heard anything about Sean being hurt. What happened?"

Marty told her about the attempted murder, the desire of The Money Club to keep it from being publicized, and the fact that the police had closed the case.

"How badly was he hurt?" she asked, tears welling up in her eyes.

"Enough that he's in the hospital. He should be released within a day or so. I visited him yesterday, and I think he's recovering quite well."

"You said you're a friend of his. What is your relationship with him?" Maddie asked.

"Maddie, if I may call you that, as I told you, I was one of two people who discovered him after the attempted murder. It bothered me that the police were doing nothing about it. My husband is the head of the Palms Springs Police Detective Unit, and I've helped my husband several times with his cases.

"My husband is out of town attending a conference, and I decided to see what I could do to help Sean. I was, and am, concerned that whoever tried to murder him will try again when they find out they weren't successful the first time. I suppose that's one of the positive things about the news blackout regarding Sean. Whoever did it may not know they were unsuccessful."

Maddie was quiet for a long time and then said, "Are you aware that Sean and I are estranged. and he's no longer living here?"

"Yes, he told me. He also asked me to tell you that his affair with Tina was the stupidest thing he's ever done in his life. He told me that he'd give everything he has to replay that part his life, and that all he wants is to be married to you and be a father to Rickie. 'I love Maddie. I've always loved Maddie.' Those were the exact words he said to me when I talked to him."

As Marty spoke, the tears that Maddie had been holding back, fell down her cheeks. "I still can't believe his affair happened. I don't know what I did wrong. I tried to be the best wife and mother possible, and it wasn't enough."

"I don't know about that, Maddie, but what I do know is he seemed very, very honest in wanting to reconcile with you. It was apparent to me that this situation is tearing him apart."

"I just can't get those pictures of him and that woman, Tina, out of my mind. I don't know how he could do something like that to Rickie and me."

"I don't know anything about any pictures, and Sean never mentioned any. What are you talking about?"

Maddie stood up and began to pace the room, tears coursing down her cheeks. After a few moments, she stopped and looked at Marty. "I hired a private investigator. I heard about him from one of the women in my yoga class. I met with him and told him that I suspected my husband of having an affair."

"Why did you suspect Sean of having an affair?" Marty asked.

"I suppose what would be called the usual things. He began, as he told me, having to work late which he'd never done before. A couple of times I thought I could smell the scent of a perfume that wasn't mine on him. We seemed to be arguing a lot."

"What was your arrangement with the private investigator?"

"I paid him a retainer fee of $5,000 and gave him information about Sean such as where he worked, a photograph of him so he could see what Sean looked like, what kind of a car he drove, things like that. He told me he would follow Sean for a week and if he found out he was having an affair, he would get photographs of Sean and the woman."

"From what you said, I'm gathering he did."

"Yes. They made me sick. Literally. After he gave them to me, I came home and threw up, and then I burned them. I knew that my life, and my daughter's, as we had known it, was over. All because of Sean and that woman."

"Maddie, I'm not saying that reconciling with Sean would be easy. In fact, it may be the hardest thing you'll ever do, but before you do anything drastic, would you at least talk to him? I know he's tried to call you, but he tells me you've changed your telephone numbers."

"First thing I did after I finished throwing up and burning the photographs was call a locksmith to change the locks on the house. The next thing I did was change my telephone numbers. I never wanted to see or talk to Sean again."

"And now?" Marty asked.

"I've missed him. When I saw those photographs, I never thought I'd say that, but I do. If it wasn't for them, I might consider a reconciliation for Rickie's sake."

"Maddie, my first husband cheated on me, but he went on to marry his secretary, so I'll never know if we'd tried to reconcile our differences, if it would have worked. My husband wasn't like Sean, who wants nothing more than to make your marriage work.

"I know it's none of my business, but you might give him a call and think about reconciling. If it doesn't work out, at least you'll never have to wonder if you should have tried. I think you might prefer that to spending the rest of your life ruing a decision you'd made because of some photographs.

"You have his telephone number. I think if you give him a call, it would dramatically speed up his healing process, and remember, he has no way of getting in touch with you. He misses you and Rickie."

Tears again filled Maddie's eyes as she said, "All Rickie does is ask me when Daddy's coming home. I haven't told her yet that he's never coming back."

"Maybe the reason you haven't told her is because maybe, just maybe, he might be coming back. Anyway, think about it."

"I will. Actually, I'm going to give him a call. I don't want it on my conscience that he didn't heal because of me. It will probably be the hardest thing I've ever done, but for Rickie's sake, I can do it."

"For your sake as well as for Sean's, too."

"Thank you for coming by here today. From what you've told me, I'm not sure I ever would have found out that he'd been hurt. This must have been difficult for you, and I want you to know I appreciate it."

"I'm happy I could be of help. I'll think good thoughts for your family, and I hope to hear that while everything will never be perfect, at least they will be better for Sean and you and Rickie. Here's my card. When you have a little time in a couple of weeks, I'd like to know what happens."

"I will. You know, after talking to you, I actually feel hopeful for the first time in weeks."

"I'm sure there will be some rough sailing, but remember those words when you hit them. One more question. I'm just tying up loose ends. What was the name of your private investigator?"

"Ryder Tait. As I said, he came highly recommended. As a matter of fact, he's called me several times just to check on me and see how I'm doing. I thought that was quite thoughtful."

"Yes, it certainly was. Well, go get your daughter, and I'll look forward to hearing from you."

On her way to her car, Marty couldn't get the thought out of her mind that it was very strange for a private investigator to call one of his clients back just to see how she was doing, and several times at that. She made a mental note to ask Jeff if he'd ever heard of that happening.

CHAPTER TWENTY-FIVE

Promptly at 3:25, Marty pulled into the strip mall where the fitness club, Workout Addicts, was located in La Quinta, just off Highway 111. Even if Marty hadn't been looking for it, she couldn't have missed the screaming bright orange sign with the club's name written prominently on it in red. It was placed in the grassy median between the parking lot and the highway.

She parked her car and opened the red front door with the words "Workout Addicts" written in large orange letters, a reversal of the colors of the sign in the median. She walked over to a muscular young man at the reception counter and said, "Hi. My name is Marty Combs, and I have an appointment at 3:30 with Bob."

"Sure, I'll give him a call and tell him you're here. He should be out in just a minute. If you want, you can have a seat over there," he said, gesturing to a row of red canvas-backed chairs with the club's name embossed on the backs in orange.

"I will," Marty said as she walked over and sat down, remembering that she'd read once how important colors were in marketing. If you wanted to create a sense of calm, you decorated with pink, violet, or blue. Conversely, red and orange were the colors one used to promote exercise or action.

Whoever decorated this was definitely aware that those colors promote what the club's selling, she thought, as she looked through the floor-to-ceiling glass walls separating the reception area from the workout room whose alternate walls were painted in red and orange, and where a number of men and women were engaged in all types of intense workouts.

A very large muscular man wearing an orange tank top and red shorts walked out of the workout room and said, "Marty, I'm Bob. Let's go back to my office. It's a little quieter there. Please follow me."

They walked through the large room where people were working with weights, jump ropes, and other equipment as well as what looked like trainers encouraging them.

Bob opened a door in the orange wall and walked down the hall to the last door and opened it for her. "My office is here, because it's the quietest place in the club. You've come here at the slowest time of day. Imagine the noise level in the early evening. It's deafening."

He sat behind a large glass desk with a state-of-the-art computer monitor on it. "I understand you asked about Kevin Summers. How can I help you?"

"Bob, I'm an antique and art appraiser. I've been hired to conduct an appraisal where Kevin works. I understand that he's the assistant manager there, and I was told he was the one who wrote the checks for some of the items that I have to appraise.

"If he could tell me what he paid for some of the things I'm appraising, it would save me a lot of time researching them, but I can't seem to reach him. He gave me a telephone number, but it's been disconnected. Can you help me get in touch with him?"

Bob was quiet for several moments, then he said, "I wish I could, believe me, I wish I could. Kevin owes my club a bundle. You see, the Workout Addicts fitness clubs are franchises, so in addition to being the manager, I'm the owner. Anyway, he's behind three months in his dues, and I haven't seen him for several days."

"From the way you said that, I'm taking it that he's usually a pretty regular member."

"I wouldn't use the word regular. I'd use the word obsessed. He was here seven days a week for 1 ½ hours. He's probably been my best member as far as attendance, but lately I've had a couple of problems with him."

"Could you share them with me? Maybe that would give me some clue as to how I could get in touch with him," Marty asked.

"I doubt it, but in addition to owing me money I had to get rid of one of my best trainers because of Kevin, although it was probably a blessing in disguise."

"What happened?"

"We have full dressing rooms with showers and everything. One evening I was in the bathroom and I overheard a conversation between Kevin and Duke, one of my trainers. The gist of it was that Duke told Kevin he owed him over $5,000 for sports bets he'd made with Duke. Duke told him if he didn't pay, he wouldn't be responsible for what might happen to Kevin."

"So essentially, he threatened him."

"Yes. I certainly didn't like that, but I was even more concerned that Duke was taking bets, in other words he was a bookie. Marty, I don't really care what people do on their own time, but he was obviously taking bets at my club. I've spent a lot of blood, sweat, and tears to get enough money together to purchase this franchise, and I'll be darned if I'm going to have it closed down because I have a trainer who's a bookie."

"I don't blame you. What did you do?"

"I fired Duke on the spot and told Kevin he had one week to pay me what he owed me, or he would no longer be welcome at Workout Addicts," Bob said.

"How did he take it?"

"Fairly well. He apologized and said he had something working for him, and he was certain he could get the money to me within that time frame. That was the last I heard from him. Like you, I tried his phone, but as you said, the number has been disconnected."

"Well, he hasn't been at work, and he hasn't been here. I wonder if he's left town? Would you happen to have an address for him? I'd like to see if any of his neighbors know anything."

"Sure. Give me a minute," Bob said as he turned his chair around and opened a filing cabinet. He leafed through his files for a moment and then pulled one out.

"Here it is. On his original application to be a member, he wrote his address down as 247 Blanca Street in La Quinta. From the way he talked, I don't think it's very far from here. If you do find something out, would you give me a call? I'm curious, too."

"I will, and thanks for your time. I hope you get your money back from him, although from the number of people I saw when we walked through the exercise room, I don't think it will be a problem if he doesn't pay you what he owes you."

"No, it won't, and for that I'm very lucky. But with me, it's more the principle of the matter. I feel like a sucker for letting him get three months behind. I should have done something about it after the first month. Oh well, now I know," he said as he stood up and walked over to the door.

"Good luck, Bob, although as I said, I don't think you'll need it."

"Thanks. I'm very lucky, and I know it."

Marty walked through the exercise room to get to the front door and noticed that there were twice as many people in it as there had been when she went in to see Bob.

She wondered if it would increase her appraisal business if she started wearing just oranges and reds, then she thought of what Carl would say, and decided that was probably not a good idea.

CHAPTER TWENTY-SIX

Marty got in her car and typed in the address Bob had given her for Kevin on her GPS. *Bob was right*, she thought. *Kevin's address is only a few minutes away from the Workout Addicts.*

Several minutes later she saw that the address she was looking for was a very attractive two-story Spanish style apartment building. It was shaped in a box like form with the side and back parts of the building housing the apartments. The front of the building was covered in red and purple bougainvillea plants. Through the key card gate she could see a swimming pool and a profusion of plants.

She walked up to the gate and pressed a button that said "Manager." A moment later a voice said, "May I help you?"

"Yes, I'm looking for Kevin Summers. I understand he lives here."

"Technically, that would be correct. However, he's three months past due on his rent, and I haven't even seen him for the last week. Your guess is as good as mine as to whether or not he lives here," the manager said.

"Oh. Would it be possible for me to see if his neighbors know where he might be? I won't be long."

"Sure, be my guest. His apartment is number 24, midway upstairs on the left. If they tell you where he is, let me know, so I can get in touch with him."

A moment later the gate opened, and Marty walked into the colorful central courtyard. The landscaping was immaculate. There wasn't even a leaf on the ground. She climbed the stairs, walked to apartment number 24, and rang the doorbell. She didn't expect him to be there, and she wasn't surprised when there was no response.

The drapes had been drawn, and she couldn't see what was or was not inside the apartment. She wondered if the apartments were furnished, because it would be difficult to move out of one of the apartments without the manager knowing about it.

She walked next door to apartment 22 and knocked on that door. Again, there was no answer, although, since the drapes were open, it was very easy to see in the window. She didn't see any movement, so she walked to the other side of Kevin's apartment, to apartment number 26.

Again, she knocked and again, there was no answer. The drapes in this apartment were closed, and she assumed that whoever lived there was working.

Well, so much for that idea, she thought. *Guess I might as well go back to the compound. This really has been a rather fruitless day.*

As she was getting ready to walk down the stairs, the door on apartment 26 opened and a woman stuck her head out. "Were you looking for me?" she asked.

"In a way," Marty said. "I'm really looking for Kevin Summers. I believe he's your neighbor. I was wondering if you'd seen him lately."

"Not lately. He came over a few days ago and told me he had to leave town for a while. He asked if I'd take care of his cat while he was gone, because he knows I love cats, and I'm always talking about getting one."

"Did you?"

"Yes, Snookums is here now, but I haven't heard from Kevin since he left. I thought he'd at least call me and check on Snookums. Kind of weird, but something has been off about him lately."

"What do you mean, off?" Marty asked.

"Well, when he first moved in here, he was a really nice guy. We used to get together for dinner once and a while. He'd cook or I would. No big deal, no romance, just friends. Then, about six months ago, something changed. He was nervous all the time and twice in the last month, a couple of guys I'd call goons, for lack of a better description, came to his apartment."

"Was he in his apartment when they came?"

"No. I saw them through the slit in my drapes. I figured if they knocked, there was no way I was going to answer my door. They were really scary looking."

"How did he seem when he asked you to take Snookums?" Marty asked.

"Really, really nervous. I heard him leave about an hour after that. I peeked out my window, you know, curious. He had a duffel bag and that was it. If you want my opinion, I think he's gone."

"What do you mean, gone?"

"Like in not coming back."

"I see," Marty said. She thought for a moment and then said, "Do you know if he had any lady friends?"

"He did at one time. He told me the ladies loved him, but he liked to love them and leave them. Said he'd never found one he was interested enough in to ask over to his apartment. If you ask me, I think he was embarrassed about where he lived."

"Why do you think that?"

"I'm a swap meet junkie, and I can recognize something fake from a mile away. Let's put it this way, when you're wearing a fake Rolex and fake Allen Edmonds Park Avenue Cap-Toe Oxfords, you want people to think you're bucks up. These apartments are nice, but not exactly ones that someone who was bucks up would rent. Know what I mean?"

"Yes, I do. Thank you so much for taking the time to talk to me. You've been very helpful. I'd like you to take my card and if you do hear from him, would you give me a call?"

"Sure. Happy to. Guess the good news is that I now have a cat. Wonder when the manager will clear out his apartment?"

"I have no idea. Oh, I just thought of something. Are these apartments furnished?"

"Yes, that's one of the good things about them. They're great for people like me, who are just starting out."

"I can see where they would be. Well, nice talking to you. Thanks again."

From everything I've heard today, sounds like Kevin has skipped town. Since he owes people a lot of money, along with what his neighbor said about scary people knocking on his door, it makes me think there's a good chance he's gone. If he was involved in gambling at the fitness center, he might owe other people as well, people who would be a lot more assertive than Duke and Bob.

CHAPTER TWENTY-SEVEN

When Marty arrived at the compound, she saw Jeff's car and thought that was strange. He'd told her he wouldn't be home until tomorrow evening. She wondered if there was a problem.

She petted Duke and Patron as she opened the gate and waved to everyone, including Jeff, sitting at the courtyard table. "Back in a minute. Let me put this stuff away," she said.

As she sat down at the table, Jeff looked at her and said, "I know. You're wondering why I'm home early. The others asked as well, but I wanted to wait until you were here, so I didn't have to repeat myself."

"Yes, I am. I was really surprised when I saw your car in the driveway. Is everything okay?"

"I think it is. Here's what happened. This morning I got a call from the chief, my boss. He's the one who made the decision to close the case regarding Sean Holmes. The chief told me he'd been uncomfortable with his decision ever since he'd been pressured to make it."

"Good. I hope he couldn't sleep. That was a lousy decision," Les said.

"Agreed, Les, but he's making it right."

"What do you mean?" Laura asked.

"Last night his wife overheard a conversation between the chief and Jerry Jessup regarding the status of Sean Holmes. When he hung up, his wife said he'd never told her about the case. He said that was because it was closed.

"From what he told me when his wife found out he'd closed the case and wasn't even looking for the would-be murderer, she went ballistic. Told him he'd sworn to protect the people, yada, yada, yada. Then he said she told him she'd leave him if he didn't reopen the case and do what was right. He said they went to bed not speaking and that neither one of them probably got ten minutes of sleep.

"The more he thought about it, he agreed with her. He was caving in to the money people, rather than doing what was right. When they got up this morning, he told her he was reopening the case, but there was a good chance he wouldn't be reelected, and she said she didn't care. She told him that having an unemployed principled husband was better than having an employed unprincipled husband."

"Wow," Marty said. "That took a lot of courage on both of their parts. Where do you come in?"

"You are talking to the lead investigator in the Sean Holmes case. The chief yanked me out of the conference in Los Angeles, had me come back here to Palm Springs, and assigned the case to me. And I'm sorry, Marty, this might not help your appraisal business once The Money Club finds out that I'm the lead investigator and that I'm married to you."

Marty was quiet for a minute and then said, "I agree with the chief's wife. I'd rather be principled and unemployed than unprincipled and employed."

"Glad you agree with my decision, not that I really had one. So, Marty, since this is now my case, what did you find out today?"

"Yeah, I've been waiting all day to hear the latest," John said.

"Okay, I had several meetings, but none that resulted in finding a suspect." She told them about Tina, Maddie, and her attempts to get information on Kevin Summers."

When she was finished, Jeff said, "I think I can help you there, Marty."

She turned to him. "You found out something about him?"

"Yes. We were able to get some credit card information on him, and he was in Las Vegas the morning of the attempted murder. He was actually charging his breakfast at one of the hotels there about the time of the attempted murder, so he's officially off the suspect list. Not to say he's a great guy or anything like that, but he isn't the person who tried to kill Sean Holmes."

"Darn. Sure would have been easier if he had been," Marty said.

"I know, but it is what it is, and in this case, it isn't, if you get what I mean."

"Okay. Well, I think we've pretty much burned through the list of suspects. What now?" Marty asked.

"We go back to square one. I'll interview Sean tomorrow and see what we've missed. It's a fact that someone tried to murder him. We'll start at square one and go from there. Something's been overlooked."

"Jeff, I'm really glad you're on this," Marty said. "I'm not a trained professional like you are. I've just been asking questions of people that seemed like they might have had some reason to get rid of Sean. I'll be honest. Right now all I'm feeling is frustrated and discouraged."

"Don't be. You did all the legwork and found out things that will help me immeasurably. Believe me, you've saved me hours. Even if you haven't identified someone as the would-be murderer, you've done a great job."

Marty's phone rang and as she stood up to walk to the far end of the courtyard to answer it, she excused herself.

"While she's gone, Max and I will get dinner," John said. "Maybe that will make Marty feel better."

"Are ya' kiddin', John? Lamb chops, spinach frittata, and a salad with garlic bread would make the most depressed person in the world feel better. Back in a few, guys," Max said.

They could see Marty animatedly talking and after about five minutes she walked back to the table, a smile on her face.

"Well, it looks like something good happened today, and since I played a part in it, I feel pretty good."

"I'll bite," Jeff said. "After all the discouraging talk earlier, we all could use something uplifting."

"I think I better wait until John and Max get back out here. You know how they like to be in on things," she said.

"Manna from my kitchen. I'm particularly interested in what you think of the frittata. I'm thinking I can serve it at the Red Pony. Enjoy!" John said as he and Max set out large platters of food for his fellow compound residents.

For several moments no one spoke as they helped themselves to John's food and began eating. Les was the first to speak. "John, Max, not only is this one of the prettiest meals you've ever served, it's absolutely excellent. I just hope there are a lot of leftovers tomorrow for lunch, since I'll be the only one here."

"Hate to disappoint you, Les," Jeff said, "but from the way this food is disappearing, not only does John have another hit on his hands with the frittata, but I'm personally going to make sure that not one lamb chop is left."

He turned to face John and Max. "Compliments to the chefs, or whichever one of you cooked this. It's delicious!"

"Wish I could claim the credit, but as usual, it's all John. I jes' do the cuttin' and choppin' for him," Max said.

"Glad you like it," John said with a smile. He turned to Marty. "Okay, time for us to hear what you learned on that telephone call you just had. From the look of the smile on your face, it must have been some good news.

Marty took a sip of her wine and then said, "That was Maddie, Sean's wife. I told you about my conversation with her earlier today. Well, she called Sean, and they've decided to reconcile. She was crying she was so happy about it. He's being released day after tomorrow. She's going to pick him up at the hospital and take him home."

"I'm glad," Laura said. "From what you've told me, Marty, they both sound like nice people."

Marty continued. "Maddie also told me they've decided to go to marriage counseling, because they really want the reconciliation to work. She said they need to figure out what led to Sean feeling that he needed to have the affair, and she needs to work through her anger about it. She feels maybe she was so wrapped up in Rickie and being the best mom around that she paid more attention to that than she did her husband."

"Wouldn't be the first marriage like that," Jeff said. "I do feel sorry for Sean. Poor guy's been through a lot lately."

"That's true, Jeff," Laura said. "But remember, he's the one who made the choice to have the affair with Tina. I'm getting some feelings that although the affair isn't the reason someone tried to murder him, it's certainly plays a part in it."

Jeff turned towards her and asked, "Anything else, Laura. Anything that would help me?"

"No, not really. I just see some darkness around his affair with Tina, but it's kind off to the side, like it's not exactly the affair that caused his would-be murder, but it was involved."

"Swell. I have no idea where to go with that."

"Don't blame you, nor do I," Laura said. "If something else comes to me, I'll let you know."

"And on that note, it's time for me to take the dogs out for the last walk of the night. If I'm going to solve this thing, I need my beauty sleep. Marty, are you about ready?" Jeff asked.

"I am," she said standing up. "John, thanks again for spoiling us. See you all tomorrow."

*****

When Marty and Jeff were getting ready for bed she said, "Jeff, I forgot to tell you something, and it's bothering me."

"What's that?" he asked as he walked into the bathroom to put his shirt in the clothes hamper.

"When I was at Maddie's this morning, she mentioned that the private investigator she'd hired, the one who took the pictures of Tina and Sean, had called her several times to see how she was doing. I thought that was strange."

"Couldn't agree more. I think that's very strange," Jeff said as he walked back into the bedroom.

"That's not all. When I talked to Maddie this evening, she mentioned that he'd called again and after asking how she was doing, said something like 'Someday you'll be happy with what I did for you.' Seems a little odd to me."

"Not a little odd. Strikes me as almost being sinister. Do you know the PI's name?"

"Yes. I asked Maddie. His name is Ryder Tait. I asked her where she'd heard about him, and she told me from someone in her yoga class."

"Let me run a search on him and see what I come up with. For some reason that name rings a bell with me, but that's about it, just a very faint bell."

CHAPTER TWENTY-EIGHT

The next morning, Jeff rolled over and lightly kissed Marty. "Good morning, my love. I need to go in early and get started on the Holmes case. If my chief and my wife are in danger of losing their incomes, I need to see what I can do to forestall that. Solving this case would be a huge step in the right direction."

"Go get 'em, tiger. Since I'd cleared my schedule for today so I could continue the appraisal which is now on hold, I have absolutely nothing that needs to be done this morning, I'm going back to sleep. Call me later and let me know what you find out about Ryder Tait."

"Will do. I have a niggle in the back of my mind about him, but darned if I can bring it up. Hopefully it will come back to me once I start researching him. Stay in bed and enjoy. I'll feed the dogs and walk them. Loves."

The last thing Marty heard as she drifted off to sleep was the sound of Jeff's shower. Two hours later she woke up and decided to start the morning with some of John's leftover cake from a couple of nights ago that she'd confiscated, and a cup of coffee while she read the paper.

Thoroughly enjoying the solitude and quietness of the compound with everyone gone, her reverie was disturbed by the ringing of her phone. Looking down at the monitor, she saw it was Carl.

"Good morning, Carl. Since my appraisal was cancelled and there's absolutely nothing that I have to do today, I'm simply enjoying my coffee and reading the morning paper. How about you?"

"I'm here at the shop a little early. Since the appraisal was cancelled, I was hoping you could come by the shop. I have something I want to show you. Any chance you could pop by? I'd even buy you a cup of coffee."

"Sounds good, and you've certainly piqued my interest. I need to shower and dress. I can be there in an hour. Would that work?"

"Sure would, and trust me, you don't want to miss what I'm going to show you."

"On that note, I'll be there as fast as I can. See you in a few," Marty said as she put her paper in the recycle bin, rinsed her coffee cup, and put it in the dishwasher. She hurried through her shower, kept her makeup to a minimum, and threw on some jeans and a t-shirt.

Thirty minutes later she was standing in front of Carl's shop, knocking on the door. It was still a half hour before his shop opened. A moment later the door was opened by Carl, who was grinning from ear to ear.

"Carl, what's going on? You're smiling like the cat who ate the canary."

"Just come with me. Now close your eyes. That's it. Hold onto my arm. We're going back to my office. Do not open your eyes. I repeat, do not open them."

She heard the door to his office close and he said, "Marty, I want you to sit down in this chair. Don't worry. I've got you, and once again, I repeat, do not open your eyes. I'm going to put something in your lap, and trust me, you'll like it. Are you ready?"

"About as ready as I'll ever be when someone tells me they're going to put something in my lap and I have no idea what it is, to say nothing of still having my eyes closed. Okay, go ahead."

"Voilà, meet Miss Simone, or Miss S, as I call her. You can open your eyes now."

Marty felt something warm on her lap as she opened her eyes. Looking down she saw a little bundle of apricot-colored fur in her lap with two big black button eyes staring at her. She picked up the little puppy and held it against her shoulder, as if she was holding a baby.

"Carl, this is about the cutest thing I've ever seen. I'm assuming she's yours, but I thought you were opposed to having a dog because of your allergies. I don't think I know the breed. What is she?"

"She's a Maltipoo, and that breed is pretty much hypoallergenic. I was at one of my client's homes helping her with the placement of some stunning Art Deco furniture pieces. Her dog had just given birth to four puppies. I took one look at them and told my client I had to have this one. It was an instant connection of the heart."

"What are you going to do with her when you're at work?" Marty asked, letting the puppy lick her cheek.

"Look over here. Here's Miss S's bed. What do you think of it?"

Marty looked to where he was pointing and saw a wicker vintage baby bassinet with an apricot colored silk sheet in it. Little apricot bows had been tied to the wicker.

"Carl, I saw that bassinet the last time I was in here. Are you really going to let your dog sleep in a vintage bassinet in your shop?"

"No, she's going to sleep in it here in my office. That's where her toys will be. I just got her last night. I think for the first time I'm in love. I know what I'm going to tell you next will sound silly to you, but I'm just so excited."

"Carl, nothing you tell me will surprise me."

"Well, I found this store online that makes matching outfits for dogs and their owners. This is going to be so fun. Miss S and I are going to start dressing alike, except for some very feminine things I'll have to get her. After all, as the owner of the best antique store in Palm Springs, I do have an image I have to live up to."

"Uh, huh," Marty said with visions of Carl and Miss S in matching outfits. Her mind boggled.

"Oh, look," Carl said, "her little eyes just closed. It's time for me to give her a bottle and then put her down for a nap."

"Carl, she's a dog, not a human."

"Bite thy tongue, Marty. This is close as I'm ever going to get to having a baby, so for a little while she will be a baby. Ohh, I'm just dreading those teen years. I hear they can be terrible."

"Well Carl, in that case, don't blink or you'll miss them. I've read where at the end of the dog's first year, the dog is about age fifteen in human years, so you'll be in those years before you know it."

"Oh, I just wish I could avoid all of it and keep her like this," he said as he fed her the bottle. "I just love this stage, and I can't wait until I get the clothes I ordered. This has absolutely given me a new lease on life. By the way, I've been meaning to ask you, how are you doing with The Money Club case?"

"Well, it's changed a bit. The chief has decided to reopen the case, even if it means he won't be reelected, and Jeff has been named as the lead detective on it. Since the case is no longer private, I can tell you what I've found out in the last couple of days."

Carl listened to Marty while he fed Miss S and then put her down for her nap. Marty privately wondered if he was going to bring out diapers after she left, but she thought that might be better left unsaid.

When she'd finished, he said, "Sounds like you've covered a lot of ground, but unfortunately no one looks like the would-be murderer.

Now that my daughter is asleep, will you join me in another cup of coffee?"

"Sure. At least she sleeps soundly. I've never had children, but I hear that's a good thing."

"Well, I did take her out twice last night, just in case. She was so good. I think I won the Maltipoo gene pool when I got her, you know, beautiful, brilliant, and so smart."

"I think you did, Carl. I think you did."

"Marty, you mentioned that Maddie and her husband are going to reconcile. That must be difficult for her."

"I'm sure it will be. I suppose it doesn't help that the man she hired as a private investigator has been calling her asking how she's doing. She told me every time he calls it's like she's reliving everything again, particularly the photographs she'd like to forget about."

"Isn't that kind of unusual? I mean I've only heard of that once, and it was a real scary guy. One of my clients hired a private investigator and after he'd found out that her husband was cheating on her, he kept calling her. He even went to her home several times and threatened her if she wouldn't start seeing him. She finally had to hire an attorney and get a restraining order against him."

Good grief, Marty thought, *that kind of sounds like what Maddie's experience has been with her private investigator.*

"Carl, I know this is a longshot, but by any chance do you remember what the guy's name was?"

"Yeah, it's etched on my brain. I thought it was a cool name for a rotten guy. Name's Ryder Tait. Sounds like the hero in a movie."

"Carl, that's the name of the private investigator Maddie hired, the one who's been calling her."

CHAPTER TWENTY-NINE

Marty got in her car and pulled her phone out of her purse, noticing that she'd had a phone call from Maddie while she'd been in Carl's shop.

Hmm, she thought, *I wonder why I didn't hear it when she called. Even though it was in my purse, I usually hear it when someone calls.* That's when she realized that the ringer had been inadvertently turned off. She turned it back on.

She pressed call back and a moment later Maddie's voice came on the line. "Thanks for getting back to me, Marty, and I'm sorry I called you, but I just didn't know who else to turn to."

"No problem. What's going on?"

"Well, I'm sure it's nothing, but you may remember that I mentioned that the private investigator I hired has been calling me. Well, last night he called me twice, and I just got another call from him. This one disturbed me."

"Why? What did he say?" Marty asked.

"He said how much he liked me and that he wanted to see me again because I was so pretty. The next thing he said scared me," she said as she began to cry.

"Take your time, Maddie. I'm not going anywhere. When you're ready, tell me what he said."

"He said, he said, now that Sean was dead, I was going to need a man around. I asked him what he was talking about, and he told me not to play coy with him, because he knew Sean was dead, even if he hadn't seen it anywhere on the news."

"Maddie, I was just getting ready to call my husband, who is now the lead detective in this case. The chief has reopened the case, so I'm sure Sean's would-be murderer will be caught within the next few days."

"Marty, I'm not finished. He told me he had a few things to do this morning and then he was coming to my home about 1:00 this afternoon so we could make plans. I asked him what kind of plans and he laughed and said, 'You know, the kind lovers make.'

"Marty, believe me, I don't know what's going on with this guy. I never led him on. I paid him a retainer fee to find out if Sean was cheating on me. You know the rest. I'm so scared. I don't know what to do."

"Let me give my husband a call, and I'll get back to you in a few minutes. Just stay put, okay?"

"I will. Thanks," she said as she ended the call.

A moment later the voice on the other end of the phone said, "Well, sleepyhead, how is your day treating you?"

"Very well, but there's a potential problem, and I think since you're now the lead detective on the Holmes case, you'll know what to do."

"Shoot."

"I just got off the phone with Maddie Holmes, and here's what she told me." Marty told him about the phone calls Maddie had received from Ryder as well as the fact that he was planning on being at her home at 1:00 that afternoon to talk about making plans, the kind lovers make. Then she told him what Carl had told her about Ryder and his client's restraining order against Ryder.

"Marty, I was just about to call you. I ran a check on Tait this morning and it's not good. He was arrested several times for assault and battery about fifteen years ago, but he was never convicted for a number of reasons. He was living in Los Angeles at the time.

"He moved to Palm Springs and worked for a couple of private investigators in the area. He went out on his own several years ago. There have been several complaints about him, but nothing ever came of them. However, what I found out just a little while ago makes me think that he's Sean's would-be murderer."

"What's that?" she asked.

"I've been bothered that because the case was closed so quickly, none of the employees at The Money Club had been properly investigated. I went over there and talked to several of them. None of them knew anything.

"Here's the interesting part. The person who was on the gate the morning of Sean's would-be murder had just been hired and it was his first day on the job. I had the photographs of everyone we considered a suspect and just before I left the police station, I'd put Ryder's photo in the envelope."

"I think I can guess what happened. The guard recognized the photo."

"Yes, he recognized the photo. He specifically remembered Ryder because he'd told the guard he was a private investigator that the president of the club had hired to protect Sean, because threats had been made against him. Ryder had asked the guard where he could find Sean, and he told him."

"Wow, so he can put Ryder at The Money Club at the time of the crime."

"Yes. I'd bet anything he's the one who did it."

"How did Ryder get away afterwards? Did he go out the gate?"

"Yes, and it was probably a very smart move, considering it was about the only way out without getting electrocuted on the fence. He just waved goodbye to the guard and said Sean had talked to the president while he was there, and they made a joint decision he wasn't needed.

"This is kind of a weird case of things falling in place. If the chief hadn't decided to reopen the case, I never would have gone to The Money Club and interviewed people. If I hadn't gone there, no one would have ever known that Ryder had been on the premises that morning."

"Are you going to arrest him for attempted murder?" Marty asked.

"I can't. Believe me, I'd like nothing better than that, but I don't have enough evidence. What I am going to do is take a couple of my deputies to Maddie's house. Once I get there, I'll decide how I want to proceed. Would you call her and tell her we'll be there about noon? I want to get things in place early."

"Sure, I'll call her right now. I think I'd only be in the way if I went over there, so I'll go back home and wait to hear what happens."

"Wish me luck. I really want this guy. And if I could solve this attempted murder in less than twenty-four hours, that would sure make me look good."

"I'll wait for your call, and good luck."

*****

"Hi, Maddie, it's Marty. I just talked to my husband, and he has good reason to believe that Ryder is the one who made the attempt on Sean's life. He'll be coming to your house about noon with a couple of his deputies. He said he wasn't sure how he was going to handle this, and that's why he wanted to be there well in advance of when Ryder said he'd be there."

"Oh no, he really thinks Ryder is the one who did that to Sean? But why? I don't think Sean ever met him, and I only met him twice, once when I paid him the retainer and once when he gave me the photographs."

"Based on some information I received earlier today, this isn't the first time Ryder has tried to develop a relationship with a client after he found out the client's husband had been cheating. Guess he thinks that the wife is vulnerable during that time."

"Marty, I'm scared. What if Ryder tries to kill me?"

"He won't. He doesn't have any reason to. Just follow Jeff's directions. With Jeff there you'll be perfectly safe. You couldn't ask for anyone better during a crisis. I thought about being there with you, but not only would I get in the way, it might interfere with whatever Jeff has planned."

"I don't know. I'd feel a lot better if you were with me."

"Thanks, but you'll be fine. Good luck, and I know everything will work out."

CHAPTER THIRTY

As Marty drove out of Palm Springs towards her compound, she looked through the gates as she passed by Casa Flores. All was quiet. The purple and pink bougainvilleas that had been planted in front of the fence and fronted the street were in full bloom and spectacular.

When she pulled into the compound driveway, she saw Patron and Duke in their usual places, next to the gate, waiting for her. "Come on guys, time you went for a little walk." Marty led them out into the desert where they searched for living things to pounce on and finally communed with nature.

When she entered the courtyard, it was quiet. Les had a note on his door which read "Painting. Please don't disturb." The other compound members were at work, and she had the place pretty much to herself. Since there were still no "have-to-do's" on her plate, she decided to spend the afternoon reading on a chaise in the courtyard.

*****

A few minutes before noon, Jeff walked through the open gate at Maddie's home and knocked on the door, his two deputies behind him. The door was immediately opened by a woman he assumed was Maddie Holmes.

"Hello, Mrs. Holmes, I'm Detective Combs. You've met my wife,

Marty, and I'm aware of the situation with Riley Tait. This is Deputy Lawson, and this is Deputy Mead. They're going to help me today. I've been thinking about this situation, and here's what I want to do, but I'm going to need you to cooperate."

"Not a problem. Just tell me what you want me to do."

Jeff gave her very explicit instructions and then he and his men spent the next half hour planting recording devices in several places in the living room and the great room.

When they were finished, Jeff said, "I'll be in the closet in your bedroom. Deputy Lawson will be next to the sliding door of the great room, and Deputy Mead will be next to the kitchen door. Naturally they will be standing to the sides of the doors. All of us have listening devices on, and once we get what we need, you saying what I told you earlier, we'll arrest him."

"But what if something goes wrong?" Maddie asked in a frightened voice.

"Nothing will, trust me. However, if there's even a hint that you could be in danger, we'll arrest him then and there. Your safety is the top priority of all three of us. Any questions before we assume our positions and I turn on the recording devices?"

"Just one. What if he talks longer than the time on your recording device, and you can't pick up what you need?"

"He won't. These devices are good for ten hours, and there is no way he can talk that long. Anything else?" Jeff asked.

"I'm sure you hid your cars," Maddie said.

"Yes, there is no way he can possibly know that we're here. This isn't the first time we've done this." He looked at his watch and said, "It's 12:45. He could be early. Time for us to go. Maddie, you'll be fine. Don't worry. Okay guys, let's do this."

The three of them went to their agreed upon positions. Promptly at 1:00 the doorbell rang and Maddie answered it. "Hello, Ryder, come in," she said.

They heard her perfectly through their listening devices. "I like your home, Maddie," Ryder said and Jeff assumed he was looking around. "I could be real happy here."

"Would you like some iced tea?" Maddie asked. "It will only take me a minute."

"Yes. So how much did you get in life insurance?" he asked as he followed her into the kitchen.

"What do you mean, life insurance?" she asked.

"The life insurance you got because of Sean's death."

"Oh, I haven't looked into it yet. There's been so much to do. Let's go back to the great room. We can talk there."

"Well, I'd rather go into the bedroom, but I guess that will do for now."

Jeff put his hand on his gun. He knew what Ryder intended to do after the conversation was over, and he wanted to be ready for him.

"Ryder," Maddie said, "you never told me how you knew that Sean had died."

"Honey, he didn't just die. He was murdered, but you knew that."

"How would I possibly know that?"

"Well, darlin', the whole reason I murdered Sean was because I know you wanted him murdered. Remember when we met at Starbucks, and I gave you the photographs? Well, you asked if I ever did anything that was a little to the left of legal, if you know what I mean."

"Ryder, I never asked you to murder Sean."

"Not in so many words, darlin', but I know what you meant. Anyway, he's dead, we're alive, and I'm looking forward to the two of us being together. Aren't you?"

"Well, it will probably take me a little while to adjust to everything, Ryder. This last week has been a bit much for me."

"Yeah, I can understand that. You know, the only thing I was worried about was getting into that club where Sean worked, but it was a piece of cake. I made up some cock and bull story, and the guard bought it. Anyway, I'm glad I killed Sean.

"Man who cheats on his wife like he did doesn't deserve to live. Yeah, life is for the living. So Maddie, what do you say that you and I go in the bedroom and get to know each other. I know you haven't said anything, but I could see it in your eyes when we met at Starbucks. I know you wanted me."

"Ryder, I think it may be a little too soon," Maddie said. Jeff could tell from the tone of her voice that she was getting nervous.

"Nah, darlin', we'll just have a little fun. Kind of a prelim for the main event in a couple of weeks. No reason we can't get married. Not like we need to ask permission of anyone. Now, where's your bedroom? Exploring a woman's body is always a little more enjoyable when we're lying on a bed."

"It's this way," Maddie said. Jeff could hear their voices getting closer. He was behind the closet door, waiting.

Maddie led Ryder into the bedroom and as soon as Ryder was in the room, Jeff threw the closet door open and shouted "Police, hands up."

Ryder whirled around, pulling a gun from his pocket. Jeff never thought, he just fired his gun, hitting Ryder's hand, and causing the gun to fly out of his hand and land on the floor. Both of the deputies had run into the room and Deputy Mead grabbed the gun on the floor.

"Ryder Tait, you're under arrest for the attempted murder of Sean Holmes." He turned to his deputy and said, "Cuff him and Mirandize him."

"Wait a minute. You said attempted murder. I thought Sean was dead."

"Sorry to disappoint you, but you didn't kill him. He's alive and in the hospital. As a matter of fact, he's expected to make a full recovery and Maddie and Sean are reconciling."

*****

Marty had been reading for about an hour when she heard the gate open. She looked up and saw her sister. "Laura, it's only 1:30. What are you doing home so early? Get some kind of vibe about Jeff meeting the suspected would-be murderer at Maddie's house?"

Patron stood up and went over to her, the hair on his back standing on end.

"Probably. I picked up that something was going on with that case, and I was too nervous to stay in my office. I told Dick I had to take the afternoon off. I must not have looked too good, because he didn't even question me. How long has Patron been like this?" she asked.

"About one minute," Marty said. "He must be picking up some vibe from you, because he's been fine until now."

"Have you heard from Jeff?" Laura asked.

"No, should I?" Marty responded.

"You will in a few minutes. Don't worry. He's okay, and yes, I think Patron is picking something up from me. I'll calm him down.

Patron, come." Laura bent down and began to whisper to the big dog. Within a minute, he was calmly lying by her side.

"I don't know what kind of miracle mumbo-jumbo stuff you say to him, but it sure works," Marty said, as her phone began to ring. She picked it up and listened for a moment, then she said, "Thank God it's you, Jeff. I've been sitting here trying to read, and I'm on the same page that I was on when I started. All I could think about was what was happening at Maddie's house."

She was quiet for a few minutes, listening to him. "Sure. I'll let everyone know that you'll give us all the details at dinner. How is Maddie holding up?"

She listened to Jeff and then said, "Tell her I said you'd make sure nothing happened to her, and so you did. And tell her the nightmare is over and she can get her life back together, and Jeff, I'm so glad you're okay. I love you."

EPILOGUE

Two months had gone by and the compound residents were gathered for their evening ritual dinner along with sharing the events of the day.

"Marty," Les said, "you were so instrumental in helping Jeff with the Holmes case. For some reason I was thinking about that today and wondering whatever happened to the people involved. He turned towards Jeff, "Any updates from either one of you?"

"Marty, I defer to you," Jeff said.

"Funny you should ask. I spoke with Maddie today and the reconciliation has gone very well. She and Sean have been in marital counseling, and she said they've gotten a lot of positive things out of it. Sean has really been working on his issues, but she feels responsible for his would-be murder.

"She told me that she was so angry when she'd seen the photographs, Ryder might have gotten the impression she wanted Sean murdered. She said she was working through that with the counselor, but she wasn't sure she could ever get over the guilt she felt."

"I can give you the update on Ryder," Jeff said. "He pled not guilty, which is pretty normal, and he's awaiting trial. Even though he's never been convicted of anything in the past, I have every reason to believe he'll be serving a number of years in prison."

"I have a question. What about the redhead Sean was involved with? I forget her name," Laura said.

"I know about her," Marty said. "Her name's Tina. Carl told me that she'd started coming into his shop to buy antiques because she was getting married and her husband, who is quite wealthy, asked her to furnish the new home they're buying with antiques."

"Wow," Laura said. "She always seems to land on her feet. Didn't take her long to find someone else."

"From what Carl told me, when you look like she does, there are a lot of older men in the Palm Springs area who are more than happy to have arm candy like Tina."

"And the real rich guy. I think his name was Basil something or other. What about him?" John asked.

"Maddie said Sean had told her he'd dropped out of the club. He sold his Malibu mansion, his horses, and his vineyard, and went back to Boston to work in his father's insurance company."

"His father wants to retire and insisted that Basil return to Boston. Something about how he'd sown enough wild oats on the West Coast, and it was time for him to settle down and assume his rightful place in his lineage."

Wonder if he's going to take his photograph collection with him? And he may find his trips to Thailand are going to be curtailed, Marty thought.

"By the way, I finished the appraisal and just got my check from The Money Club. Carl was a huge help to me since so many of the items had been bought from his shop."

"How's he doing? I think you told me he'd bought a puppy and was outfitting the dog in clothes to match his."

"Are you serious?" Les asked. "I've never met the guy, but that seems pretty unusual."

"It may be unusual, but the last time I was there Carl and Miss S were in matching purple shirts. Carl had a multi-colored purple ascot on, and she had a matching scarf. Carl wore white pants, and Miss S had on a white skirt.

"Carl told me he felt badly because he had to tell her she couldn't wear her favorite necklace with the diamond bone as long as she had the scarf on. He said after he dresses her every morning, she goes over to her jewelry box and stands on her back legs, waiting for him to get the jewelry that matches her outfit."

The courtyard was absolutely still. Each of the compound residents, as well as Max, had a look of incredulity on their faces.

"Well," John finally said, "there's no way I can top that no matter what I serve. Back in a minute with dinner."

"John, maybe you should also bring another bottle of wine. I, for one, could sure use a glass after hearing that," Les said.

Laura looked down at Patron and said, "Patron, I know you understood every word that's been said, but Marty and Jeff are not getting you any jewelry. Just deal with it."

Woof. Woof. Woof. I wouldn't wear it even if they did, Laura heard Patron say.

RECIPES

CHANGE IT UP CAKE

Ingredients:
1 box vanilla instant pudding mix
1 ½ cups milk
1 box chocolate cake mix (I use a triple chocolate fudge cake mix.)
12 Oreo crème sandwich cookies, crushed (I put them in a plastic bag and use a meat mallet to crush them.)
½ cup semisweet chocolate chips
1 container (8 oz.) frozen whipped cream topping, thawed
Cooking spray

Directions:
Heat oven to 350 degrees. Spray bottom and sides of 9" x 13" pan with cooking spray. In a large bowl beat pudding mix and milk together for 2 minutes. Stir in cake mix and 1 cup of crushed cookies until combined. Spread batter evenly in pan. Spread chocolate chips on top.

Bake 30-35 minutes (ovens vary so it may need more time) until a toothpick inserted in center of cake comes out clean. Cool completely in pan.

Spoon and spread whipped topping evenly over top of cooled cake. Sprinkle with remaining crushed cookies. Store covered in refrigerator until ready to serve.

NOTE: It's called Change It Up Cake because that's what you can do. Butterscotch chips, pudding, cake, and Nutter Butter cookies. Or try lemon flavors, or mix and match. I've tried this recipe a number of different ways and it's always a hit!

BEST BARBECUE COLESLAW

Ingredients:
16 oz. pre-shredded tri-color coleslaw mix (Refrigerated section of market.)
½ cup mayonnaise
2 ¼ tbsp. milk
2 ¼ tbsp. buttermilk
1 ¼ tbsp. apple cider vinegar
1 ¾ tbsp. lemon or lime juice
¼ cup white sugar
Salt and freshly ground pepper to taste
Optional: 1 small Jalapeno pepper, deseeded and finely chopped

Directions:
In a large mixing bowl, combine the coleslaw mix, and if using, jalapeno pepper. In a small bowl whisk together the mayonnaise, milk, buttermilk, apple cider vinegar, and lemon or lime juice until smooth. Add the sugar, salt, and black pepper to the liquid mixture. Whisk until combined. Cover the coleslaw mix and the dressing with plastic wrap and refrigerate.

About ten minutes before it's time to serve the coleslaw, plate the coleslaw and pour the desired amount of the mayonnaise mixture over the cabbage mixture. Serve and enjoy!

ROASTED GARLIC BUTTER

Ingredients:
½ cup butter at room temperature
½ shallot, finely minced
1 large head garlic
2 tsp of dry BBQ steak seasoning rub
1 tsp. olive oil
Tin foil
Plastic wrap

Directions:
Heat oven to 400 degrees. Cut the top ¼ off the head of garlic and discard. Place the bottom, cut side up, on a large square of tin foil. Brush the olive oil over the exposed cut garlic. Fold the tin foil around the garlic and tightly seal. Bake for 1 hour. Remove from oven, let cool 2-3 minutes, then squeeze or pull cooked garlic cloves from the garlic hull and set aside.

In a small bowl, combine the softened butter, shallot, roasted garlic cloves, and steak rub. Spread mixture onto plastic wrap and mold into a log shape. Wrap the plastic wrap around it. Store in refrigerator for a couple of hours.

When ready to use, slice log into 1" thick rounds and place on meat or fish of your choice. Enjoy!

SPINACH FRITTATA

Ingredients:
10 oz. baby spinach, washed, stems removed & chopped
2 tbsp. olive oil
1 medium onion, chopped
2 large garlic cloves, chopped
9 large eggs
2 tbsp. milk
1/3 cup Parmesan cheese, shredded

3 tbsp. sun-dried tomatoes, chopped
Salt & pepper to taste
3 oz. goat cheese, cut into pieces

Directions:
Preheat oven to 400 degrees. In medium size bowl whisk together eggs, milk, Parmesan cheese, sun-dried tomatoes. Add salt and pepper to taste

Sauté onion in olive oil in ovenproof frying pan over medium heat, about 4-5 minutes. Add garlic and cook 1 more minute. Add spinach. Spread evenly on skillet bottom. Pour egg mixture over spinach & cook on medium-high.

Use a spatula to lift up the spinach mixture along the sides of the pan to let egg mixture flow underneath. Sprinkle goat cheese over top of mixture when it is partially set.

Place frying pan in oven & bake for 13-15 minutes, until frittata is fluffy and golden brown. Remove from oven, let cool for several minutes. Cut into quarters and serve. Enjoy!

BERRY PUDDING CAKE WITH MACADAMIA CARAMEL SAUCE

Ingredients:
Pudding:
8 cups cooked cornbread, crumbled
3 cups mixed berries, your choice
2 cups heavy cream
8 large egg yolks
1 cup plus 2 tbsp. sugar
2 tbsp. vanilla
1 to 2 tbsp. cold unsalted butter, cut into bits

Sauce:
¼ cup unsalted butter

1 cup chopped macadamia nuts
1 cup firmly packed brown sugar
1 cup heavy cream
Nonstick cooking spray

Directions:

Preheat the oven to 350 degrees. Coat a 9" x 13" baking dish with nonstick cooking spray. Combine the cornbread and berries in a bowl.

In another bowl whisk together the cream, egg yolks, 1 cup of sugar, and the vanilla. Pour the mixture over the cornbread and berries and stir well to combine and coat. Let soak for a few minutes until some of the liquid is absorbed, then transfer to prepared dish. Sprinkle the top with the remaining 2 tablespoons of sugar and dot with butter.

Bake the pudding until puffy and pale golden brown, 40-55 minutes. Let rest for 10 minutes.

Sauce:

Melt the butter in a large saucepan over medium heat. Add the nuts and toast in the butter for 2 to 3 minutes. Add brown sugar and stir until melted. Add heavy cream. Bring to a boil and remove from heat.

Assembly:

Cut the pudding cake into squares, spoon on sauce, and serve. Enjoy!

LEAVE A REVIEW

I'd really appreciate it you could take a few seconds and leave a review of Missing in the Islands.

Just go to the link below. Thank you so much, it means a lot to me ~ Dianne

http://getbook.at/MCLUB

Paperbacks & Ebooks for FREE

Go to www.dianneharman.com/freepaperback.html and get your FREE copies of Dianne's books and favorite recipes immediately by signing up for her newsletter.

Once you've signed up for her newsletter you're eligible to win three paperbacks. One lucky winner is picked every week. Hurry before the offer ends!

ABOUT THE AUTHOR

Dianne lives in Huntington Beach, California, with her husband, Tom, a former California State Senator, and her boxer dog, Kelly. Her passions are cooking, reading, and dogs, so whenever she has a little free time, you can either find her in the kitchen, playing with Kelly in the back yard, or curled up with the latest book she's reading. Her award-winning books include:

Cedar Bay Cozy Mystery Series

Cedar Bay Cozy Mystery Series - Boxed Set

Liz Lucas Cozy Mystery Series

Liz Lucas Cozy Mystery Series - Boxed Set

High Desert Cozy Mystery Series

High Desert Cozy Mystery Series - Boxed Set

Northwest Cozy Mystery Series

Northwest Cozy Mystery Series - Boxed Set

Midwest Cozy Mystery Series

Midwest Cozy Mystery Series - Boxed Set

Cottonwood Springs Cozy Mystery Series

Cottonwood Springs Cozy Mystery Series – Boxed Set

Coyote Series

Midlife Journey Series

Red Zero Series

Black Dot Series

The Holly Lewis Mystery Series

Newsletter

If you would like to be notified of her latest releases please go to www.dianneharman.com and sign up for her newsletter.

Website: www.dianneharman.com,
Blog: www.dianneharman.com/blog
Email: dianne@dianneharman.com

PUBLISHING 10/11/19

MISSING IN THE ISLANDS

BOOK NINE OF

THE MIDWEST COZY MYSTERY SERIES

http://getbook.at/MITI

A bad business deal

An unfaithful husband

A hacked computer

A sick child

A death – but was it?

Those are the things that take Kat and Blaine to the Caribbean. Some people think it's a great place for a vacation, but as they quickly find out, it's not just tropical drinks and sitting in the sun.

If someone wants to get lost in the islands, it can be pretty hard to find them. Good thing there's a pitbull and a fast speedboat to help.

This is the eighth book in the Midwest Cozy Mystery Series by two-time USA Today Bestselling Author, Dianne Harman.

Open your smartphone, point and shoot at the QR code below. You will be taken to Amazon where you can pre-order 'Missing in the Islands'.

(Download the QR code app onto your smartphone from the iTunes or Google Play store in order to read the QR code below.)

Made in the
USA
Middletown, DE